"[A] stunning new book…Told i   -
ries are both mesmerizing and pa

                                                        e

"Captures that peculiar nexus of hormones, deprivation, and political imperative on a Northern Irish child coming of age."
—Susan Salter Reynolds, *Los Angeles Times Book Review*

"There is no denying the discipline that has gone into *Everything in This Country Must.*"
—Charles Taylor, *The New York Times Book Review*

"McCann has the knack of capturing the intensity of these strongly held views in a low-key prose that underscores their vitriol and in a way that disturbs the reader's sensibilities."
—*Richmond Times-Dispatch*

"Masterful. These emotionally charged, beautifully controlled tales can only enhance McCann's already considerable reputation."
—*Kirkus Reviews* (starred review)

"These are powerful stories—gritty, memorable, and ambitious. The novella goes straight to the heart, both in terms of its theme and its emotional punch."
—Edna O'Brien, author of *Wild Decembers*

"Beautifully, poetically written…The need to read them over and over again can't be denied."   —*Booklist*

"Colum McCann's stories are brooding, meditative, and lyrically controlled to that delicate point where the emotion within them intensifies with each succeeding reading and recognition. The political turmoil of Northern Ireland finds here an answering, subtly respondent voice—wonderfully skilled and deeply felt."
—Seamus Deane, author of *Reading in the Dark*

"Further evidence of McCann's remarkable gifts as a prose artist as well as storyteller…In each of these pieces, the miracle is how McCann, with prose so terse and spare, is able to create worlds so emotionally complex and moving."   —*Library Journal*

Also by Colum McCann

This Side of Brightness
Fishing the Sloe-Black River
Songdogs

EVERYTHING IN THIS COUNTRY MUST

A Novella and Two Stories

Colum McCann

Picador
Henry Holt and Company
New York

Picador® is a U.S. registered trademark and is used by Henry Holt and Company under license from Pan Books Limited.

For information on Picador Reading Group Guides, as well as ordering, please contact the Trade Marketing department at St. Martin's Press.
Phone: 1-800-221-7945 extension 763
Fax: 212-677-7456
E-mail: trademarketing@stmartins.com

"Everything in This Country Must" first appeared in *The Atlantic,* a section of "Hunger Strike" in *GQ,* and a version of "Wood" in *The New Yorker.*

Designed by Lucy Albanese

Library of Congress Cataloging-in-Publication Data

McCann, Colum.
    Everything in this country must : a novella and two stories / Colum McCann.
        p. cm.
    ISBN 0-312-27318-5
    1. Northern Ireland—Social life and customs—Fiction. 2. Social conflict—Northern Ireland—Fiction. I. Title.

PR6063.C335E93 2000
823'.914—dc21   99-43614
                                                                                CIP

First published in the United States by Metropolitan Books, an imprint of Henry Holt and Company, LLC

10 9 8

FOR

Isabella and John Michael

Horses buried for years
Under the foundations
Give their earthen floors
The ease of trampolines.

PAUL MULDOON
Dancers at the Moy

Contents

EVERYTHING IN
THIS COUNTRY
MUST

A SUMMER FLOOD CAME and our draft horse got caught in the river. The river smashed against stones and the sound of it to me was like the turning of locks. It was silage time and the water smelled of grass. The draft horse, Father's favorite, had stepped in the river for a sniff maybe and she was caught, couldn't move, her foreleg trapped between rocks. Father found her and called *Katie!* above the wailing of the rain. I was in the barn waiting for drips on my tongue from the ceiling hole. I ran out past the farmhouse into the field. At the river the horse stared wild through the rain maybe she remembered me. Father moved slow and scared like someone traveling deep in snow except there was no snow, just flood, and Father was frightened of water, always frightened. Father told me *Out on the rock there, girl*. He gave me the length of rope with the harness clip and I knew what to do. I am taller than Father since my last birthday, fifteen. I stretched wide like love and put one foot on the rock in the river middle and one hand on the tree branch above it and swung out over the river flood.

Behind me Father said *Careful now, hai*. The water ran warm and fast and I held the tree branch, still able to lean down from the rock and put the rope to the halter of the lovely draft horse.

The trees bent down to the river in a whispering and they hung their long shadows over the water and the horse jerked quick and sudden and I felt there would be a dying, but I pulled the rope up to keep her neck above water, only just.

Father was shouting *Hold the rope, girl!* and I could see his teeth clenched and his eyes wide and all the big veins in his neck, the same as when he walks the ditches of our farm, many cows, hedgerows, fences. Father is always full of fright for the losing of Mammy and Fiachra and now his horse, his favorite, a big Belgian mare that cut soil in the fields long ago.

The river split at the rock and jumped fast into sprays coming up above my feet into my dress. But I held tight to the rope, held it like Father sometimes holds his last Sweet Afton at mealtime before prayers. Father was shouting *Keep it there, girl, good!* He was looking at the water as if Mammy was there, as if Fiachra was there, and he gulped air and he went down in the water to free the draft horse's hoof, and he was gone so long he made me wail to the sky for being alone. He kept a strong hold of one tree root but all the rest of his body went away under the quick brown water.

The night had started stars. They were up through the branches. The river was spraying in them.

Father came up spluttering for air with his eyes all horsewild and his cap lost down the river. The rope was jumping in my hands and burning like oven rings, and he was shouting *Hold it girl hold it, hai, for the love of God hold it please!*

Father went down in the water again but came up early, no longer enough in his lungs to keep down. He stayed in the river holding the root and the water was hitting his shoulders and he was sad watching the draft horse drown, so I pulled hard on the halter rope and the horse gave a big scream and her head rose up again.

One more try, Father said in a sad voice like his voice over Mammy's and Fiachra's coffins long ago.

FATHER DIPPED UNDER and he stayed down as long as yesterday's yesterday, and then some headlights came sweeping up the town road. The lights made a painting of the rain way up high and they put shadows on the hedgerows and ditches. Father's head popped out of the water and he was breathing heavy, so he didn't see the lights. His chest was wide and jumping. He looked at the draft horse and then at me. I pointed up the road and he turned in the flood and stared. Father smiled, maybe thinking it was Mack Devlin with his milk truck or Molly coming home from the sweet shop or someone come to help save his favorite horse. He dragged on the tree root and struggled out from the river and stood on the bank and his arms went up in the air like he was waving, shouting *Over here over here, hai!*

Father's shirt was wet under his overalls and it was very white when the headlights hit it. The lights got closer and in the brightening we heard shouts and then the voices came clear. They sounded like they had swallowed things I never swallowed.

I looked at Father and he looked at me all of a sudden with the strangest of faces, like he was lost, like he was punched, like he was the river cap floating, like he was a big tree all alone and desperate for forest. They shouted out *Hey mate what's goin' on?* in their strange way and Father said *Nothing* and his head dropped way low to his chest and he looked across the river at me and I think what he was telling me was *Drop the rope girl,* but I didn't. I kept it tight, holding the draft horse's neck above the water, and all the time Father was saying but not saying *Drop it please Katie, drop it, let her drown.*

THEY CAME RIGHT QUICK through the hedge with no regard for their uniforms and I could hear the thorns ripping back against their jackets. One took off his helmet while he was running and his hair was the color of winter ice. One had a mustache that looked like long grasses and one had a scar on his cheek like the bottom end of Father's hayknife.

Hayknife was first to the edge of the river and his rifle banged against his hip when he jumped out to the rock where I was halter holding. *Okay, luv, you're all right now,* he said to me, and his hand was rain-wet at my back. He took the halter and shouted things to the other soldiers, what to do, where to stand. He kept ahold of the halter and passed me back to Longgrasses, who caught my hand and brought me safely to the riverbank. There were six of them now, all guns and helmets. Father didn't move. His eyes were steady looking at the river, maybe seeing Mammy and Fiachra staring back at him.

One soldier was talking to him all loud and fast, but Father was like a Derry windowshop dummy, and the soldier threw up his arms and turned away through the rain and spat a big spit into the wind.

Hayknife was all balance on the rock with the halter, and he didn't even hold the branch above his head. Icehair was taking off his boots and gun and shirt and he looked not like boys from town who come to the barn for love, he looked not like Father when Father cuts hay without his shirt, no, he looked not like anybody; he was very skinny and strong with ribs like sometimes a horse has after a long day in the field. He didn't dive like I think now I would have liked him to, he just stepped into the water very slow and not show-offy and began making his way across, arms high in the air, getting lower. But the river got too deep and Hayknife was shouting from the rock, saying *Stay high, Stevie, stay high side, mate.*

And Stevie gave a thumb-up to Hayknife and then he was down under the water and the last thing was the kick of the feet.

Longgrasses was standing beside me and he put Stevie's jacket on my shoulders to warm me, but then Father came over and he pushed Longgrasses away. Father pushed hard. He was smaller than Longgrasses but Longgrasses bashed into the trunk of the tree and hit against it. Longgrasses took a big breath and stared hard at him. Father said *Leave her alone, can't you see she's just a child?* I covered my face for shame like in school when they put me in class at a special desk bigger than the rest, not the wooden ones with lifting lids, except I don't go to school anymore since what happened with Mammy and Fiachra. I felt shame like the shame of that day in school and I covered my face and peeped instead through my fingers.

Father was giving a bad look to Longgrasses. Longgrasses stared at Father for a long time too and then shook his head and walked away to the riverbank where Stevie was still down in the water.

Father's hands were on my shoulders keeping me warm and he said *It'll be all right now, love,* but I was only thinking about Stevie and how long he was under water. Hayknife was shouting at the top of his voice and staring down into the water, and I looked up and saw the big army truck coming through the hedgerow fence and the hedge was broken open with a big hole and Father screamed *No!*

The extra lights of the truck were on and they were lighting up all the river. Father screamed again *No!* but stopped when one of the soldiers stared at him. *Your horse or your bloody hedge, mate.*

Father sat down on the riverbank and said *Sit down Katie,* and I could hear in Father's voice more sadness than when he was over Mammy's and Fiachra's coffins, more sadness than the day after they were hit by the army truck down near the Glen, more sadness than the day when the judge said *Nobody is guilty, it's just a tragedy,* more sadness than even that day and all the other days that follow.

Bastards, said Father in a whisper, *bastards,* and he put his arm around me and sat watching until Stevie came up from the water, swimming against the current to stay in one place. He shouted up at Hayknife *Her leg's trapped,* and then *I'm gonna try and get the hoof out.* Stevie took four big gulps of air and Hayknife was pulling on the halter rope and the draft horse was screaming like I never heard a horse before or after. Father was quiet and I wanted to be back in the barn alone waiting for drips on my tongue. I was wearing Stevie's jacket but I was shivering and wet and cold and scared because Stevie and the draft horse were going to die since everything in this country must.

• • •

FATHER LIKES HIS TEA without bags like Mammy used to make and so there is a special way for me to make it: Put cold cold water in the kettle and only cold, then boil it, then put a small boiling water in the teapot and swish it around until the bottom of the teapot is warm. Then put in tea leaves, not bags, and then the boiling water and stir it all very slowly and put on the tea cozy and let it stew on the stove for five minutes making sure the flame is not too high so the tea cozy doesn't catch flame and burn. Then pour milk into the cups and then the tea, followed at last by the sugar all spooned around into a careful mix.

My tea fuss made the soldiers smile, even Stevie, who had a head full of blood pouring down from where the draft horse kicked him above his eye. Father's face went white when Stevie smiled but Stevie was very polite. He took a towel from me because he said he didn't want to get blood on the chair. He smiled at me two times when I put my head around the kitchen door and he held up one finger meaning *One sugar please* and a big O from fingers for *No milk please.* Some blood was drying in his hair and his eyes were bright like the sky should be, and I could feel my belly sink way down until it was there like love in the barn, and he smiled at me number three.

Everyone felt good for saving a life, even a horse life, maybe even Father, but Father was silent in the corner. He was angry at me for asking the soldiers to tea and his chin was long to his chest and there was a puddle at his feet. Everybody was towel drying except Father because there was not enough towels.

Longgrasses sat in the armchair and said *Good thing ya had heat lamps, guvnor.*

Father just nodded.

How was it under the water, Stevie? said Longgrasses.

Wet, said Stevie and everybody laughed but not Father. He stared at Stevie, then looked away.

The living room is always dark with Father grim, but it was brighter now. I liked the green of the uniforms and even the red of Stevie's blood. But Stevie's head from the horse kick must have been very sore. The other soldiers were talking about how maybe the army truck should take Stevie straight off to hospital and not get dry, just get stitches, and not get tea, just come back later to see about the draft horse if she survives under the heat lamps. But Stevie said *I'm okay, guys, it's just a scrape, I'd kill for a cuppa.*

The tea tasted good from long brewing and we had biscuits for special visitors, I fetched them from the pantry.

I bit one to make sure they were fresh and I carried out the tray.

I was sneezing but I was very careful to sneeze away from the tray so as to have politeness like Stevie. Stevie said *God bless you* in his funny funny way and we were all quiet as we sipped on the tea but I sneezed again three four five times and Hayknife said *You should change out of them wet clothes, luv.*

Father put down his teacup very heavy on the saucer and it was very quiet.

Everyone even the soldiers looked at the floor and the mantelpiece clock was ticking and Mammy's picture was staring down from the wall and Fiachra when he was playing football and the soldiers didn't see them but Father did. The long silence was longer and longer until Father called me over, *Come here, Katie,* and he stood me by the window and he took the long curtain in his hands. He turned me around and wrapped the curtain around me and he took my hair and started rubbing, not tender but hard. Father is good, he was just wanting to dry my hair because I was shivering even in Stevie's jacket. From under the curtain I could see the soldiers and I could see most of all Stevie. He sipped from his tea and smiled at me and Father coughed real loud and the clock ticked some more until Hayknife said *Here, guv, why don't you use my towel for her?*

Father said *No thanks.*

Hayknife said *Go on, guv,* and he put the towel in a ball and made to about throw it.

Father said *No!*

Stevie said *Take it easy.*

Take it easy? said Hayknife.

Maybe you should all leave, said Father.

Hayknife changed his face and threw the towel on the ground at Father's feet and Hayknife's cheeks were out-puffing and he was breathing hard and he was saying *Fat lot of fucken thanks we get from your sort, mister.*

Hayknife was up on his feet now and pointing at Father and the light shone off his boots well polished and his face was twitching so the scar looked like it was cutting his face. Longgrasses and Stevie stood up from the chairs and they were holding Hayknife back, but Hayknife was saying *Risk our fucken lives and save your fucken horse and that's all the thanks we get, eh?*

Father held me very tight with the curtain wrapped around me and he seemed scared and small and trembly. Hayknife was shouting lots and his face was red and scrunched. Stevie kept him back. Stevie's face was long and sad and I knew he knew because he kept looking at Mammy and Fiachra on the mantelpiece beside the ticking clock. Stevie dragged Hayknife out from the living room and at the kitchen door he let go. Hayknife turned over Stevie's shoulder one last time and looked at Father with his face all twisted but Stevie grabbed him again and said *Forget it mate.*

Stevie took Hayknife out through the kitchen and into the yard toward the army truck and still the rain was coming down outside and then the living room was quiet except for the clock.

I heard the engine of the army truck start.

Father stood away from me and put his head on the mantelpiece near the photos. I stayed at the window still in Stevie's jacket which Stevie forgot and he hasn't come back for yet.

I watched the truck as it went down the laneway and the red lights on the green gate as it stopped and then turned into the road past where the draft horse was lifted from the river. I didn't hear anything then, just Father starting low noises in his throat and I didn't turn from the window because I knew he would be angry for me to see him. Father was sniff sniffling, maybe he forgot I was there. It was going right down into him and it came in big gulps like I never heard before. I stayed still but Father was trembling big and fast. He took out a handkerchief and moved away from the mantelpiece. I didn't watch him because I knew he would be shamed for his crying.

The army truck was near out of sight, red lights on the hedgerows.

I heard the living room door shut, then the kitchen door, then the pantry door where Father keeps his hunting rifle, then the front door, and I heard the sound of the clicker on the rifle and him still crying going farther and farther away until the crying was gone and he must have been in the courtyard standing in the rain.

The clock on the mantelpiece sounded very loud, so did the rain, so did my breathing, and I looked out the window.

It was all near empty on the outside road and the soldiers were going around the corner away when I heard the sounds; it wasn't like bullets, it was more like pops one two three.

The clock still ticked.

It ticked and ticked and ticked.

The curtain was wet around me but I pulled it tight. I was scared, I couldn't move. I waited it seemed like forever.

When Father came in from outside I knew what it was. His face was like it was cut from a stone and he was not crying anymore and he didn't even look at me, just went to sit in the chair. He picked up his teacup and it rattled on the saucer so he put it down again and he put his face in his hands and he stayed like that. The ticking was gone from my mind and all was quiet everywhere in the world and I held the curtain like I held the sound of the bullets going into the draft horse, his favorite, in the barn, one two three, and I stood at the window in Stevie's jacket and looked and waited and still the rain kept coming down outside one two three and I was thinking oh what a small sky for so much rain.

WOOD

IT WAS JUST PAST NIGHTTIME when we brought the logs down to the mill. The storm was finished but there was snow still on the hedges and it looked like they had a white eyebrow.

Mammy drove the red tractor. It went down the lane with hardly any speed at all. The headlights were off and she kept the throttle steady so as nobody would hear. She was wrapped in two coats and I had my brown duffle closed to the neck but still the wind was cold. The logs scraped along the ground behind the tractor and made a sound like they were nervous too. The logs were wrapped with chains to keep them from slipping, but still the chains rattled and I held my breath.

The light from Daddy's room was on. It sprayed out yellow onto the snow at the back of the house.

Mammy said hush to me.

She pushed the throttle forward and the tractor quickened a little on the hill. She didn't want the engine to cut out and die. Daddy might hear something and then he would ask. The engine was like the sound of a cough rising.

Mammy turned in the tractor seat and pulled up her head scarf to look back and see if all the logs were following. I was walking behind the logs and I gave her a wave and she smiled and turned again.

My boots made footprints in the tracks left by the pulled wood. They were size eights that belonged once to Daddy and still they were much too big for me and I could feel the newspaper shifting in the toes.

The snow had frozen and it crunched under my feet.

The tractor got to the top of the hill and then, when the logs came up, Mammy pulled back on the throttle.

All the clouds had disappeared and there was a slice of moon out that looked like a coin had been tossed in the sky. I wanted to sit on the end of the logs and have the tractor skid me along. We had a small wooden cart before Daddy got sick and he skidded us through the fields on the back of a rope. We laughed and shouted hard, me and my brothers. Sometimes he dragged us along through the mud, all the way down to the church where we had services. Once he pulled the cart too hard and we slammed into a tree. I got a big cut on my head and it bled down my chin, but I didn't go to the hospital. Daddy said I was a big enough lad, not to cry, and he carried me all the way home. He had wide shoulders then, not hunched into himself like an old raven.

THE MAN WITH THE BIG CAR had called at the door three days before. He had gray hair and a gray suit and a Union Jack in his lapel. His face was very tight like someone had squished it together with pliers. I knew him from church, but couldn't remember his name. He said that there'd been a fire in the Lodge and it was an emergency, he didn't want to use the Kavanagh mill on the other side of town.

Forty poles, he said to Mammy. Twenty-five shillings each. They'll be carrying the banners. We'll leave the wood at the end of the laneway. They'll have to be smooth and varnished and rounded at the top.

I was sure that Mammy was going to say no thanks. Ever since Daddy got sick she said no thanks to every other job, she said we got enough money from the checks in the post. But this time she rubbed her hands together and finally she whispered, Okay.

Your husband'll be all right with that, then? he asked.

He will, aye.

He was never mad keen before, was he?

Mammy looked behind as if she was expecting Daddy to be listening, then she jiggled the door handle up and down.

The man smiled and said, Next week, so?

Aye, next week, said Mammy.

I LOOKED UP TO THE LIGHT in Daddy's window and then back to the tractor. Mammy had her hands held hard now to the steering wheel as she turned the corner going close to the house.

There was ivy on the walls and it looked like our secret was climbing up the vines to Daddy's room.

I ran to catch up with the logs in the courtyard. My chest rose and fell hard. Mammy was leaning back over the seat and waving her arms at me to hurry up. She was trying to say a word but there was no word coming and then she whipped her body back around.

She stood up quickly from the tractor seat and turned the steering wheel hard left and braked. I was thinking maybe she had hit one of the dogs, but I ran around the side and saw the wheelbarrow, full of bricks. The back wheel of the tractor had just missed it. It would have made a fierce noise. I grabbed ahold of the wheelbarrow and rolled it away a few feet.

Mammy whispered: Get you there in front of the tractor and make sure there's nothing else in our way, good boy.

The courtyard was empty mostly but I moved the bricks to the side of the old outhouse and then I dragged some scrap planks over to the water tank. Mammy looked stiff in the face, but then she gave a smile as I cleared the path for the tractor.

The snow from the top of the planks sat on the sleeves of my coat and then melted and ran down to my elbows, where it made me shiver.

I waved Mammy on.

She put her boot down hard on the brake, releasing the lock—it clicked a loud click—and the tractor rolled forward slowly once more. The tires caught on the hard snow and the logs made a groan against the ground.

The doors to the mill were open. Mammy drove the tractor all the way in and now the sound was different, softer, the tires rolling over sawdust. I pulled the string that led to the light and it flooded the mill and there was dust all around us. A few empty bottles of lemonade were on the workbenches, where Daddy had left them long ago. I thought about running into the house to get some milk from the fridge but Mammy said: Come on now, Andrew.

She climbed down from the tractor and yanked her dress from where it caught on the mudguard. She closed the door of the mill, clapped her hands together twice, and said: Let's get cracking.

DADDY SAYS he's as good a Presbyterian as the next, always has been and always will, but it's just meanness that celebrates other people dying. He doesn't allow us to go to the marches, but I saw a picture in the newspapers once. Two men in bowler hats were carrying a banner of the King on a big white horse. The horse was stepping across a river with one hoof in the air and one hoof on the bank. The King wore fancy clothes and he had a kind face. I really liked the picture and I didn't see why Daddy got upset. Mammy never said anything about the marches. If we asked a question she said, Ask your daddy. And when we asked why, she said, Because your daddy said so.

I thought maybe our poles would hold a banner just like that, with the King sitting high up on his horse. I asked Mammy but she said, Hush now son we've got a big job to do.

. . .

I KNEW WHAT TO DO from watching Daddy. We un-
wrapped the chains from the logs. The metal links felt dead
in my fingers.

Mammy had thin little wool gloves on and she offered
them to me, but I said no thanks. She took off her head
scarf. Her hair fell to her shoulders, black with little bits of
gray. Her cheeks were red from the cold and she looked
pretty like she does in old photographs. She reached into her
dress pocket, took out some matches, went across to the
kerosene heaters.

When she struck the match it looked like there was fire
jumping from her hands. In a few minutes the mill was
heating. We pulled the last of the chains out from under the
logs and one of them rolled across the floor of the mill. It
bumped into the sawhorse.

Mammy looked out the window, but the yard was empty
except for the tracks we had left in the snow. She tapped on the
windowpane and the ice on the glass shook. Then she took
the chain saw down off the wall and said to me: Stand back.

Mammy fired it up and the metal teeth ripped around and
around the blade. She made a vee cut at first and I put pressure on the log so it would cut quicker. She sliced the log into
three long sections and there was a bead of sweat on her fore-

head, just sitting there, not quite sure if it was going to fall down her face or not, but she turned off the chain saw and put her head into her shoulder, and wiped the sweat away.

How long will it take? I asked.

A few days, she said. They need them in time for marching practice.

I saw some bats flying outside, past the window. They dipped around and went very fast.

We bent down to lift the piece of log into the cutting machine. The wood was wet where Mammy had sawed it and I could feel it ooze down my fingers.

We were breathing hard when we got the log in place. Mammy hit the switch and the sharp blade went along the middle of the log. When you cut trees you can tell how old they are by the number of rings, and I wondered if I cut myself open would I be able to tell things about myself, but I didn't say anything because Mammy was staring into the machine.

Do you think the pieces are too thick? she said.

I wasn't sure, so I said no, they were perfect.

She gave a small smile and some hair fell down her face and she tied it back behind her head. She stood with her hands on her hips.

Right so, she said.

We took the first piece to the rounding machine and Mammy spent a long time making sure that everything was adjusted right: the blades, the buttons, the oil. She looked at me across the machine for a long time and said, It's our secret, right?

Aye.

You won't tell your brothers neither?

No.

God help me, she said in a whisper.

Mammy turned the machine on. It clattered and she looked like she wanted to tell it to be quiet. The wood spun around and around and bits came flying off until it began to look like a pole. I started sweeping the floor. I put the bristles of the brush right down into the gaps of the floorboards just so I could get every little piece.

There was a great smell of timber in the air. Mammy switched off the machine and ran her fingers along the wood and then she turned to me.

Will you get the thingymajig ready there, love? she asked. She was pointing at the sanding machine. I ran across and got it. It wasn't heavy.

Plug it in there, good lad, she said.

A little spark jumped out from the wall, blue like lightning.

. . .

WE MADE ONE GOOD POLE but Mammy said it was too late, that we'd try again the next night. We reversed the tractor out and left it in the courtyard where it was before and then we put the lock on the door of the mill. Mammy took a rake to the snow on the ground to get rid of all the footprints and tire marks.

When we got back to the house I showed Mammy the secret to keeping quiet on the stairs, staying to the left-hand side, watching for the creak on the seventh step, then stepping real light on the eleventh and missing the fourteenth altogether.

Mammy washed her hands in the sink so Daddy wouldn't smell the wood and then she went in to wake him up and turn him so he wouldn't get sores on his body.

She does that six times a day. First she tucks her hands in under his legs and she props them up with a pillow. Then she puts her hand under his back and she rolls him over. The first few times she did it he used to moan but now he just grits his teeth and looks straight ahead at the wall. Once, when she was rolling him, my brothers and I saw his willy fall out from the gap in his pajamas. Paulie laughed first and then me and then Roger. Daddy looked at us and said, Get out boys. Mammy tucked his willy back in and pulled the drawstring tight.

• • •

THE DAY DADDY FELL he went down between two sawhorses. My brothers and me were playing hide-and-go-seek in the courtyard. Roger found him and shouted to come quick to the mill and I ran as fast as I could. Daddy was there with his eyes wide open. He had a piece of sandpaper in his hands and his hair was covered in dust. He was trying to move but he couldn't.

He was making chairs when it happened. Daddy made the most beautiful chairs in the whole of Britain. Any man or woman, said Mammy, would be proud to sit in one of his chairs. They were fit for the Royal Family and they were even fit for the Queen herself. He used to make cabinets too, and sometimes he even fired the little brass handles in the forge at the rear of the mill. They were mahogany cabinets, which was the most expensive wood and only made on special order from a man in Belfast. Every time he sold a cabinet Daddy would bring us to town for red lemonade and ice cream. Sometimes for fun he swayed in and out of the lines.

Daddy even made the seats in our church. He said everyone should do his bit for God. Our neighbour Mr. McCracken said the seats would put the Catholic church to shame, but Daddy said there was no shame in any church, cheap wood or good wood, everyone sat in the same direction.

Reverend Banks said in a sermon that they were great works of the Lord, and that day all the men slapped Daddy on the back and he walked out tall and proud.

He was so tall he could grab onto the rim of the door in the mill and pull himself up ten times. He worked there all day long, last star to first, and Mammy used to bring out sandwiches to him, sometimes in the evening a can of beer.

When he finished a chair Mammy always tested it out for him. Once in summer I saw her standing outside the mill on a wooden stool and she was reaching up in the air and laughing. Daddy was beside her, smiling. He used to smile a lot like that and his teeth were nice and white.

The doctor said it was a stroke and when Daddy tried to say things he couldn't. For a long time his words were all jumbled like he had too many in his mouth. He sometimes stared at his hands like they belonged to someone else.

Mammy moved into my bedroom because Daddy couldn't sleep right, and I moved in with my brothers.

The worst thing was that he wasn't able to turn the pages of his Bible anymore, but Mammy had an idea. She took out her makeup bag and put hairpins on his favorite pages so they stuck out the top. Then Daddy was able to flip the hairpins using the back of his hand, and he was happy then even though it was hard for him to smile.

Daddy has a face that, if you don't know it, you might think he's angry when he smiles, but it's like a special password, the way his mouth turns.

EACH NIGHT it was like we were digging a secret tunnel. I never stayed up so late before. We cut the logs until they were thin, smoothed them out, and made little round rims at the top, so they looked like the front of our banisters. That was the hardest part. Then we used paintbrushes to put on the preservative and even some polish so the logs would be nice and fancy and dark brown.

We used up all the kerosene and we had to work fast just to keep our fingers warm. Mammy gave me a pair of gloves, Daddy's old ones. They were yellow and I thought about the white gloves of the marching men. I could picture their nice gloves around the poles and the big shiny buttons they wear on their coats.

We made four poles the second night and seven the third. We got so fast that we made twelve on the fourth night. They kept getting better and better. The little round pieces at the top were perfect.

On the last night we finished the job early. We stacked the forty poles in the corner of the mill near the door. They were leaning together like a whole big forest all smoothed out.

Mammy ran her fingers over a couple of the poles and when she got a splinter in her hand she said, Oh, sugar.

She sanded the pole down again and then we walked back across the courtyard. She sucked the little bit of blood from her finger. It was late. There were millions of stars in the sky and the moon was smaller than before. All the snow had melted away and the ground was muddy now.

We kicked off our boots at the front door and in the kitchen we ate some bread and butter and apricot jam.

Mammy went to have a bath and I went to my room. My brothers were sleeping away. They were breathing at different paces and they were a bit like a caterpillar the way they moved. I thought about squashing them.

I didn't sleep very well. I kept tossing and turning and then I had to help Roger back to sleep because he started crying. I went downstairs to get him some hot milk but there was none left in the silver canister. Mammy was sitting there with her head in her hands. She didn't notice me until I dropped the lid of the canister and it made a big clang. She took me over to her and gave me a big kiss on the head, which made me feel silly.

I went back upstairs and missed all the creaky points.

Roger cried when he heard there was no milk but at last he went to sleep and they all started breathing again in their caterpillar way.

I pulled up the covers and made a tunnel underneath. I was thinking of what it would be like to go there just once, to see the men in bowler hats carrying the poles along the street. Lots of people cheering and blowing on whistles and drums playing. Ice-cream vans giving out free choc ices. All the crowd would stand up on the tips of their toes and say My oh my, look at that, aren't they wonderful poles, aren't they lovely?

WHEN I WOKE UP it was still dark like it always is in winter. The wind was blowing hard.

Mammy was on the landing already dressed.

We went into Daddy's room and closed the door behind us. He had the Bible open on his chest. The hairpins were sticking out. She brushed his teeth and got him to spit into the pan and then she told him I was mad keen on shaving him in the morning, was that all right?

Daddy said that would be all right as long as I didn't hack his face to pieces. He was just about able to get his words out proper.

I said, Great.

I ran downstairs and heated some water in the kitchen and then I got the white basin that was made from old china. His blade and the soap were under the sink. The towels and washcloth were already folded on the table.

I took a quick look out the window and Mammy had the poles stacked up in the center of the courtyard. She was looking down the laneway and waiting for the van to come and pick them up.

I balanced the blade across the bowl and carried the things out of the kitchen. I didn't care about the stairs anymore. I even pressed heavier so he would know I was coming. He was already waiting for me. He smelled a bit like he needed a bath. I flipped on the radio by the bed and turned it up a bit just like Mammy told me to. The news was on, there was something about queues in the petrol stations.

Daddy was propped up in the pillows and I put a towel behind his head and he gave that funny smile he has.

He said, Heated the water, did you?

I nodded and dipped a washcloth into the bowl and wet the side of his face. I was listening hard under the radio for the sound of the van coming along the laneway. There was nothing but the wind blowing outside. When his face was wet I put the soap in a lather and tried to smooth it out on his face and my fingers were a little shaky.

The radio had gone from news to ads.

I got the soap on his face and took the blade—Daddy calls it a straight blade—and started like Mammy does, at the bottom of his neck where he has all these tiny little bumps. He closed his eyes like always. The blade went slow. I didn't want to cut him, but he told me to go faster, not to worry, it was a better shave if you went quicker.

You'll do it one day soon yourself, son, he said.

I heard my brothers getting up in the room. They were shouting and laughing and hitting each other with pillows.

Daddy moved a little and some soap got on his pillow. I wiped it off, then went up along the side of his cheek to his sideburns. His eyes stayed closed. I went quickly over the left side of his face.

Good lad, he said.

I was praying the van would come soon. Music started on the radio and Daddy told me to turn it off, but I pretended I didn't hear him and kept shaving away. The black and gray hairs made funny little patterns on the blade, along with the soap. I wiped it carefully on the end of the towel.

He said, Turn the radio off, son.

I said, Ah please, Daddy.

Are you listening to your father? he said. Turn that mess off right now.

I reached across and flipped the radio off. Just then I heard the van in the laneway and he heard it too. It turned in at the gate and made a squishy sound as it went through the puddles.

I could see by the way Daddy's forehead creased that he was wondering. I told him it must be the postman coming early and I pretended to look out the window and I said, Aye it's a red van, it must be the post. Really it was a blue van. I turned the radio on again so he wouldn't hear any sounds or van doors or the poles being loaded or any other noise that might happen. But he told me straight to turn the radio off again, no ifs ands or buts.

I started shaving his chin and then I moved up to his mustache and thought I should have washed my hands better because maybe there was still the smell of wood and preservative on my fingers.

My hands got very trembly.

The blade touched against his top lip but it didn't bring any blood. With his eyes closed, he looked like he was thinking about something very carefully.

They're very early, he said.

Aye.

This is the earliest I ever heard them.

The doors of the van slammed with a loud bang and I coughed a loud cough. Daddy stirred his back against the pillows and said how it must be a package of some sort, but for the life of him he couldn't imagine who would be sending a package.

I don't know, Daddy, I said.

He asked me to help run his fingers over his face, so I lifted his hand up. We started first on the neck, then the cheeks, the sideburns, down to his chin, and then I helped him touch the little hollow between his chin and his mouth.

You missed a part, he said to me.

Will I shave it?

No, run downstairs, he said, see about that package.

I bolted down. Mammy was still in the courtyard when I got outside. She had tucked the money away in her apron. The van was gone. My brothers opened the window upstairs and they were roaring down, but I didn't hear what they were saying.

Mammy, I said.

Aye?

He thinks there's a package.

Mammy went across the yard, taking small steps through the puddles.

I looked at the oak trees behind the mill. They were going mad in the wind. The trunks were big and solid and fat, but the branches were slapping each other around like people.

HUNGER
STRIKE

THE BOY WATCHED from the headland above the town. He saw the old couple as they took the yellow kayak out from the house. They shunted it with difficulty to their shoulders and carried it toward the pier.

The old woman walked at the rear. The man was slightly bent, but he was still a good foot taller than she. She held the boat as high above her head as she could, but still it sloped down toward her. Their faces were lost beneath shadow as they shuffled down the tarmac road. Between them, resting on either shoulder, were the paddles. As they walked, the man and woman seemed like some strange and lovely insect.

When they got to the edge of the pier they shucked the yellow kayak from their shoulders and busied themselves with getting it to water.

It was low tide, so they used long ropes to drop the boat from the pier. It landed with hardly a ripple. They stood talking a moment and the sunlight shone through their clothes, giving darkness to the shape of their bodies.

She was rake-thin and the old man carried a paunch.

The old man made a gesture toward the sea and then turned and held on to the rungs as he climbed down the pier's rusted ladder. Even in his slowness he was fluid. He planted himself firmly in the kayak and placed the paddle across the center to stop the boat from rocking. The woman followed down the ladder tentatively. A breeze caught her dress and the old man touched her on the back of her legs. She turned and seemed to let out a small laugh as he guided her from the ladder into the double well of the boat. When she placed her foot down, the kayak hiccuped in the water.

They wore no life jackets but the man fumbled with a spray skirt, adjusting it tightly to the lip of the well. He nudged his paddle against the wall of the pier and the boat began to move out into the harbor. His paddle hit the water, sending out ripples that had long faded before she too reached out and struck, now in unison with him.

The kayak glided out and the boy's eyes followed them all the way until they turned and moved south along the headland, a bright yellow speck on the gray cloth of the sea.

SO THIS, THEN, was the Galway town where his mother had once spent her summers: sunlight, steeples, green postboxes, the stark applause of seagulls, the mountains stretching in the distance like a gift of simplicity.

THE BOY PULLED on an extra shirt—it had once been his father's—and inside there was still room for a whole boy more. He rolled the sleeves high on his forearms and crumpled the collar so that it wouldn't look ironed. Across the caravan his mother was still sleeping. Her chest rose and fell. Her hair had fallen over her face and some of the strands had taken on the rhythm of her breathing, lifting and falling. The boy stepped across the linoleum floor with his shoes in his hands and he opened the door quickly to stop it from creaking.

Outside, the last spits of rain had just died on the wind.

On the cinder block doorstep he put on his shoes and looked out at the sea. The gray horizon bled into the gray sky so that he could not tell where the sky began and the sea finished. Only a single fishing boat broke the expanse.

Moving away from the caravan, he kicked at a few stray stones. He wore black drainpipes hitched high on his hips, exposing white socks and black shoes. The boy had not polished his shoes since he bought them and they were scuffed now like dark ice.

He followed the track that meandered muddily down the slope, steadying himself on tree branches until he reached the main road into town. It was still narrower than most other roads he had ever known. In Derry he had never been allowed to wander, but his mother said this town was safe, she knew all its nooks and crannies, it was a harmless place.

The rain had ripened the roadside grass and the boy reached the graveyard, where someone had placed a small china Virgin near a headstone. He wandered through the cemetery, patting his shirt pocket where he had a near-empty box of cigarettes stolen from his mother's handbag. Hunching under his jacket, he lit a cigarette and then spat near a crucifix. He felt a sudden shame rise to his cheeks, but he spat again at another gravestone and walked on. He was thirteen years old and it was the fourth cigarette of his life. It tasted cruel and lovely and it made his head spin. He smoked it down to the filter, put it between his thumb and forefinger, then flicked it high out over the stone wall of the graveyard. It fizzled red through the air and the suggestion of it remained on his tongue like morning breath as he walked around the graveyard, past all the curious wreaths and statues and carvings. He looked at the names and dates on the stones, many of which were covered now with long grasses and lichen.

At one of the stones he saw an empty pint glass with lipstick on the rim and, when he looked closely, he saw that it belonged to the grave of a young man not much older than himself.

Tough shite, he said to the stone.

He turned and hopped the stile in the wall, rejoining the road toward town. The road had no markings but he balanced along an imaginary white line that twisted and curved around the corners, switchbacking once so he thought he might come around and meet himself.

A car passed him and beeped and the boy wasn't sure if it was a greeting or a warning. He waved back weakly and stuck to the grass verge as the road cantered down the hillside into the town. He stopped and looked at the sign that gave the name of the town in two languages—he could not make the connection between them, the English being one word, the Irish being two. He tried to juggle the words into each other but they would not fit.

A few men stood brooding and malignant outside a

pub at the bottom of the hill. The boy nodded at them but they didn't gesture back.

How're you? he said to nobody, under his breath.

Oh, flying.

And yourself?

Sound enough.

He thought to himself that he wore a shirt of aloneness and he liked this idea; he pulled it around himself as he walked for hours past quiet shops, beyond a boarded-up blacksmith's, along a row of lime-colored bungalows, through a barren football field, over the high wall of a handball alley, then back to town, where he came to a small amusement arcade full of rude and tinny noise.

This is a stickup, he said to a machine.

He pulled a cigarette from his shirt pocket without removing the pack—the way his uncle might once have done—and he played a single video game with the unlit cigarette hanging from his mouth. It bobbed up and down as he cursed the spaceships on the machine. On one of his fingers he had, months ago, begun to tattoo a single word but had stopped when he wasn't quite sure what the word should be. All that appeared now was a single straight line where he had stuck a hot needle into his forefinger and smudged blue ink on it.

The tattooed finger repeatedly struck the button on the

video machine and the boy was well into his third game when he simply turned, left the arcade, and strolled down to the pier.

Just outside the harbor, the yellow kayak was making its way back through the water and the old couple was paddling with surety and grace. The paddles sliced the air in rhythm and the sunlight flashed on the turning blades. Seagulls flew over and around the kayak, looking for fish, he supposed, and it seemed to the boy that the birds made hunger look easy.

HIS MOTHER HAD TOLD HIM: Do not say *wee*. Do not say *wee*. She said there was a landscape to language and their accents could be a dangerous curiosity right now. He thought to himself that he was a boy of two countries with his hands in the dark of two empty pockets. He walked along the distance of the pier and he said the word *wee* repeatedly until it meant nothing at all. It could have been a rope or a knot or a winch or perhaps even a thing of joy.

Wee, he screamed, running down from the pier and all the way along the empty beach. *Wee*.

THAT FIRST NIGHT the caravan listed and moaned in the fugue of wind that ferried itself up from the water. The caravan sat on cinder blocks, one hundred yards from the cliff face, tethered with a chain at either end. When they switched the lights on, the boy thought the whole thing must have looked like some sad and useless lighthouse.

It's stupid here, he said.

His mother turned around from the stove and said: Oh, it's not so bad. You'll see. You'll end up loving it.

Have you heard any news?

Nothing yet.

The wind lisped through the gaps in the door and carried the smell of fresh salt water. The boy took his black Swiss Army knife from his pocket and placed it on the Formica table, flipped open the blade, and tested its sharpness on a few arm hairs. He cut down close to the skin and he wondered about a freckle on his arm, what might happen if he tried to scoop it out with the knife. He began scraping at the freckle with the tip of the blade until there was a sharp jab of pain and he thought he might have drawn blood. He sucked at his forearm and tasted nothing and, without blood, was disappointed at the whim of his pain.

When he looked up, his mother had already placed a plate of beans and toast in front of him.

The boy pushed his penknife into his plate and it slid among the beans and he thought it looked like an absurd kayak in a sea of red. He lifted it up and licked the handle and began spearing individual beans. They broke at the weight of his knife until he learned to pierce them lightly, and he held them in the air, on the tip of his knife, staring at them. He didn't eat at all.

His mother sat down. She poured two mugs of tea from the pot and began eating her own meal, feigning indifference.

Through the steam that rose from the cups, he saw her face shimmy like a fun-house mirror. He began to blow air on his plate.

Is it too hot, love? she asked.

No.

It's your favorite.

I'm not hungry.

You haven't eaten all day. I bet you could eat that whole thing in, oh, two minutes flat. Less even.

You know what? he said, his voice shrill. It's stupid here.

She closed her eyes briefly and then stared out the window. The boy sliced the beans with his knife and speared the piece of toast, which was soggy now. He lifted the bread in the air and the middle section fell out and it struck him that the bread had lost its heart. It splashed in the plate and a few small dots of tomato juice spotted the table. His mother wiped them up with her finger, let out a long sigh.

We'll play chess, she said.

I don't know how.

I taught you once when you were sick. When you had the chicken pox and you were home from school. You loved it.

I don't remember that.

There's a set in the box beneath your bed.

It's not my bed.

We'll play anyway, she said. I'll teach you again.

I don't want to.

Your father was a great player, one of the best.

The boy pushed his plate away and said nothing. He watched as his mother stared down into her teacup and he could see a tear forming at the edge of her left eye. She blinked and caught it on the corner of her dress and then she rose from the table and took the four steps across the caravan toward his bed, which doubled as a sofa. Beneath it there was a cupboard. As she yanked the door open it seemed to the boy that she was pulling at the side panel of a coffin.

Dust rose up around her and she covered her eyes and coughed, then came back over to the table carrying the chess set, which was sealed with brittle tape. She pierced the tape with the prongs of her fork. One by one she took the pieces out from the box and named them as she placed them on the table: the king, the queen, the castle, the knight, the bishop, the pawns.

I don't like those wee pieces, he said.

She stared at him and then removed his plate from the table to make room for the board but he caught the side of the plate and said to her in a loud voice: No.

There was silence in the caravan until his mother forced her lips into half a smile and said that she would practice on her lonesome. She found room on the table by propping the end of the board out over the edge, so it looked like some sort of precipice. She lined the white pieces along the edge of the board, close to her stomach, and the boy was reminded of a biblical story where animals were shoved over the edge of a cliff.

She reached forward and moved one of the white pawns, then shunted a black pawn upward in the same corridor of squares. She hummed very softly. Soon the pieces were spread out all over the board.

Check, his mother said to herself.

The boy poked at his plate and saw the soggy heart of bread that lay there. He moved the lump around in the red sauce with his knife, bored at first, until it began to take shape. He mashed the bread with the tip of the blade and then saw what it could be. His father, a carpenter, had once told him a man could make anything of anything if he wanted to. The boy began to mold the bread quickly. He moved it around the plate with the knife and it soaked up more sauce, took on a definite form. He thought of his uncle in prison: a single cell, the darkness outside, the sound of boots along a metal catwalk, the carving of days into a wall.

He dropped the knife and began molding with his fingers.

IN THE LATE EVENING, when she struggled up from the sofa, he was still awake at the table and he had created a chess piece, a knight. It was stark and red from the tomato sauce it had been dunked into. She pulled up her chair to the table and smiled at him as he lowered his eyes. Holding the shaped bread, she smiled again, put her hand on his shoulder, and told him the knight looked delicious.

It's not for eating, Mammy, he said.

THE NEXT MORNING, when he waited outside the green phone box near the pierside, he found out for sure. His mother replaced the receiver and opened the door. The hinge squeaked and it sounded like a keen, and when she stepped out her face contained such sadness that she looked like she had been on a journey containing the forecast of her own death.

He's on, she said.

The boy didn't reply.

She moved to hug him but he stepped away.

I'll not go back, said his mother. They want me back but I'll not go.

I'll go back, the boy said.

You'll stay here with me.

In her voice she was saying: Please.

He stood silently and watched her scan the beach road. Some forlorn tourists stood with their hands in their pockets. A middle-aged couple hauled deck chairs from the back of their car, placed them with great deliberation on the sand, tightened their coats around themselves. A young girl was being pulled along by an anemic wolfhound. An ice-cream truck upped the volume of its song. His mother appeared to be remembering things from a shapeless past, and in her eyes she couldn't seem to make sense of how she had gotten here, this town, this street, this patch of seaside outside the phone box. She looked down at her shadow, which pooled at her feet, and she toed at the ground.

Come on, we'll go back to the caravan.

No, said the boy.

We'll make a nice cup of tea.

I don't want tea.

Come on back. We'll dump loads of sugar in it and rot our teeth to hell and sing songs into the evening. Are you on? Let's go back. Please.

Will he die, Mammy?

Of course he won't, she said.

How do you know?

I don't, she replied softly.

There's four already dead, he said.

Yes, I know.

The boy stared a moment beyond her shoulder and then bit his lip and walked away and she watched him go, his shirt moiling around him.

The sea wind blew bitter and she felt it cold at the edges of her eyes and she followed his movement, beyond the pier and up the far hillside, becoming just a small speck of white in the distance.

The boy wandered in a stupor for an hour, found himself by a barbed-wire fence. Behind the fence some sheep were daubed haphazardly with red. He flung stones at the sheep and when they scattered he twanged the barbed wire and wondered if the reverberation would connect with all other pieces of barbed wire, that the sound might carry, from fence post to fence post, all the way north to a squat gray building topped with razor wire.

Bastards, he shouted.

Later in the day, when he came back down to the town, the headline stared at the boy from the newsstands. The newspaper sported a bright purple banner but no photograph and it wasn't even the biggest headline, but he bought a copy anyway, tore out the front page, put it in his jeans pocket. He felt as if he were carrying his uncle at his hip, that he could stay alive in there and emerge when all of this was over.

The boy hopped the railing along the beach and landed soft on the sand.

In the rocks near the pier he lit a fire with the rest of the newspaper. He warmed his hands as the pages burned and curled. The smoke made his eyes water. He read through the article five times and was surprised to learn that his uncle was just twenty-five years old. He was one of four prisoners on the strike—already, for each man dead another had replaced him and the boy found it strange that the living were stepping into the bodies of the gone. The dying, he thought, could go on forever. A phrase from the newspaper rattled around in the boy's head: intent to kill. He wondered what it meant. He let it roll beneath his tongue and he thought to himself that it sounded like the title of a film he had seen once on television. For a second the boy allowed his uncle to appear on a movie poster. An explosion lit the side of his face and a black helicopter cut the air. Beneath his uncle's chin soldiers were running scared. They were moving out of the poster and his uncle's eyes followed them.

The boy had never met his uncle—his mother never visited the prison—but he'd seen photos, and in those images the face was hard and angular with shocking blue eyes, the hair curled, the eyebrows tufted, a scar running a line of outrage across the bottom of his nose.

This was the face the boy would carry with him, even though he knew it had since become bearded, the hair longer and dirty and ringleted, that before the hunger strike his uncle had worn a blanket like many of the other men, that he had once lived in a cell where they smeared their own shit on the wall in protest. There had been a picture smuggled out of the H-blocks when the dirty protest was on—a prisoner in a cell, by a window, wrapped in a dark blanket, with shit swirled in patterns on the wall behind his head. The boy wondered how anyone could live like that, shit on the walls and a floor full of piss. The men had their cells sprayed down by prison guards once a week and sometimes their bedding was so soaked they got pneumonia. When the protest failed they cleaned their cells and opted for hunger instead.

The boy poked through the ashes of the fire and tucked the article into his pocket.

There was a slowness in his walk until he reached the far hillside overlooking the pier and then he ran up the slope, making his own path through the grasses and heather.

He kicked at the heather with violence and swung his arms through the air and spat at the sky and then he lay down at the top of the hill and shoved his face into the grass. In the grass he found his uncle's face once more, and it was hard and worn and looked like it belonged in a catechism. The beard went all the way to his chest. The skin had already begun to stretch across the cheekbones with this morning's first refusal of food. His eyes seemed larger for the fact of his hunger. When the boy turned and looked up to the sky again he thought that if there really was a God he didn't like Him, he could never like Him.

He cursed aloud and his shout went out over the water—the horizon was already stained with sunset—and the water took the shout and swallowed it. He tried again. Fuck you, God.

A flock of birds rose up and over him with thin calls and he put his face to the earth once more, cursing his father, gone in an accident years ago, and now his father's brother going too.

The boy thought to himself that the uncle he didn't know was all the uncle he'd ever know.

OUTSIDE THE CHEMIST'S there was an old-style weighing machine and he stood upon it, but he didn't have a tenpenny piece so the needle didn't waver.

He punched the glass, then put his mouth to the slot where the money should go, and he reamed up a glob of phlegm and let it go. A man in the shop, working late, looked up from a small pile of pills on the counter and saw the young boy with his mouth to the machine.

The boy lifted his head suddenly, then lowered his eyes and stepped down off the weighing scales. The phlegm hung oblong from the coin slot.

He began running up the road and he could still taste the metallic residue of the coin slot on his lips. The pharmacist came to the door of the shop and watched the boy, who was spitting now on the side windows of cars as he went, stopping just once to look over his shoulder. The boy saw the pharmacist shaking his head as he went back inside, the shop bell ringing behind him. The boy gave him two fingers, then turned and ran toward the headland, where a single light burned against a window.

• • •

IN THE HIGH and lonely caravan he was exhausted by his anger and he allowed his mother to hold him in the doorway. She placed her hand on the back of his neck and there was a faint smell of sweat and perfume to her. He broke the hug and they sat silently in near darkness until she began to teach him how to play chess. At first he refused the game, but she persisted in showing him the patterns the pieces could make, the hop of the pawn, the bishop's shift sideways, the strange interchange between king and castle, the large vocabulary of the queen. He began to remember the rules and he reached for the pieces, shifting them quickly, without thought. She allowed him some vagabond moves and he slowly relaxed, his shoulders losing their tenseness. He was amazed at the way the knight moved, how brazen and complicated it was. He tried its permutations and developed an affinity for the form—the solid breathing body of a horse and yet something human too. He searched for a word he had learned in school, centaur, and held the word in his mouth.

For a long time he protected both knights, and he sat in a huff when his mother took one of them with her bishop.

A clock ticked and the generator hummed while the boy held the pout.

She rose suddenly and went to the fridge and brought out the playing piece that he had made from bread. It had hardened in the fridge and it was still red from the tomato sauce.

Here's your knight, she said.

He laughed and took it and bit a little corner of the ear and immediately felt sorry that he had marred it. The bread tasted stale in his mouth and he tongued it into the palm of his hand and remolded it to the knight. After he put the knight down on the board, he noticed that she never threatened the piece. He began to put it in situations to test her, but his mother just smiled at him and avoided it. When the board was almost depleted she suddenly gathered all the chessmen and rearranged them, careful not to smush the shaped bread with her fingers.

The boy picked up his knight. It was more pliable now that it was long out of the fridge and he had to continually wet the small piece he had bitten.

She started a new game but he coughed hard.

Why won't you talk about it? he said.

I'd rather not.

That's stupid. It's stupid here. I hate it.

His mother sighed and twisted a lock of her hair around her finger. Her hair was extraordinarily black against the whiteness of her hands.

What does political status mean anyway?

It means they say it's a war. That they're prisoners of war and they should be treated like prisoners of war. If it's not a war then they're just criminals.

Of course it's a war. Jesus.

Thatcher says it's not, so they can't get political status.

Tin-knickers?

She chuckled. Tin-knickers, aye.

He noticed that she spoke with her old northern accent and he was happy. He put the chess piece to his nose and smelled it, the tomato sauce it had been dipped into.

I'm going to write him a letter, said the boy.

He can't get letters.

Why not?

It's one of their rules.

I don't care about their rules, said the boy. I'm going to write him a letter and send it to Grandma and she'll smuggle it in for me.

And what'll you say?

I'm going to tell him how to make a chess set.

Your uncle would like that, she said.

He could use all the bread they give him.

Yes.

He could dunk it in water.

Yes he could.

He'd have lots of time. He could shape them.

He could, yeah.

She sat forward in her seat and reached across and touched his face, stroking it very tenderly with her fingers. At the touch he immediately withdrew and her hand hovered in midair and he could see that she had been biting her nails.

That's not good, he said. You won't be able to play the guitar.

Oh, she said.

She was surprised by his comment and how old he sounded, and she withdrew her hand and began once again to wrap her hair around her fingers.

Are you going to get a gig?

What's that? she asked, distracted.

Are you going to get a gig in the pub?

I'll maybe ask tomorrow.

Are we really going to stay here?

For a while anyway, maybe.

I'm sick of beans on toast.

She rolled her eyes with great exaggeration and said: It's stupid here.

He stared at her, confused, and then she jostled him on the shoulder and they both smiled.

Come on, she said, let's play another.

The boy repositioned the chessmen. His mother showed him how to play a fool's mate and after three turns he was able to stop it, using the knight that moved like a strange and unassailable drop of blood on the board. As the game went on it was still the only piece she didn't take. He learned how to protect pawns; at what time to switch the castle and the king; how to form a small army in front of his most powerful pieces; how to keep his finger on the chessman until he had made up his mind.

Does he play chess?

I don't know.

I could send him letters about it.

Yes, she said, with great sadness.

Would Grandma get them to him?

We'll have to see.

A clock ticked with painful deliberation on a small shelf above the cooker, and it seemed to the boy that each tick got louder as the night went on.

I bet he's great at chess.

Maybe he is, she said.

Did he play against Daddy?

When they were young maybe.

Who won?

I'm not so sure, love.

Why not?

Oh, Kevin, she said.

I'm just asking.

His mother allowed him to win a game and he was angry at the ease of it. She lit a cigarette and blew the smoke over his head and he craved one. When she went to put the chess set away he reached for the ashtray and took a quick pull and blew the smoke down between his knees. He fanned the air so she wouldn't see and then he rose from the table and carefully wrapped his red knight in a piece of aluminum foil from her cigarette pack. He put the knight at the back of the fridge where it was coldest, took a milk bottle from the inside shelf, and pierced the gold metal lid with his finger. He put the bottle to his mouth and drank deep. His mother turned around and watched him as the boy wiped a sleeve across his mouth.

Hey there, she said.

What?

Give me a hug.

She came across and took his shoulders, but he curved himself away from her grip and stepped outside and he could hear her sighing behind him. She called his name but he didn't turn and she went to the doorway of the caravan, watching him disappearing into the night, where a light drizzle fell. She shouted his name again.

He pulled his shirt over his head and moved farther away to a stone wall that ran like a bad suture toward the sea.

BACK HOME, there had been protests. Huge crowds lined up, carrying pictures, chanting as they made their way down the street. Once he had gone with his mother. She had held his hand, which was all right because he was still only twelve then. He could feel her nervousness and she kept her head down as she walked, watching her feet. A blue head scarf obscured most of her face. When she introduced herself to another woman she used her maiden name. The boy elbowed her. She leaned down and told him to shush or they would go right home. They moved along with the crowd, his mother sad and weary, talking to him about other marches in the sixties. They had been more hopeful, she said. There was trouble, sure, but it was a different sort of trouble, less menacing, more optimistic. She said the trouble nowadays tasted bitter.

Nobody even knows what a civil right is, she said, and her voice went high as if the past had just escaped her and she was surprised by its disappearance.

After a while, the boy didn't listen to her, just walked

along excitedly. He loved the sound of the voices around him and he carried himself with a sort of bravado. His arms swung by his side. On the ground he found a poster of the Free State with a balaclava painted on it so that the country itself seemed to have the face of a gunman. He picked the poster up and brandished it until the wind took it and it sailed back over the crowd. His mother lit her cigarettes anxiously. Down near the Diamond they heard the first rumors about petrol bombs being thrown farther on down side streets. The boy felt his fingers tingle generously at the thought of fire in the streets, but his mother grabbed his elbow and they immediately retreated home, with her dragging him so that the toes of his shoes were almost ripped by the pavement.

He had tried to dig his heels in and for the first time ever she had slapped him, lightly, on the cheek. They were standing outside a butcher's shop. It had been burned down earlier that week and a couple of charred carcasses were still hanging on hooks. The boy stared over her shoulder at the meat that dangled in midair. Her light slap still stung his cheek and then he had begun to cry and they walked the streets together, her arm around his shoulder.

At home on Casement Row she locked the door, turned off the lights, and then she began to soak a duvet in the bath as she always did, just in case.

They sat in the darkness and listened to the sounds of the street.

He could tell a Saracen just by the way the wheels sounded against the tarmac. Or the direction of a helicopter by whichever windowpanes were rattling more, front or back. He picked at the stuffing that came from the arm of the couch and secretly spat the yellow sponge across the room. Boys his age were out there, firing stones. He had developed a specific scowl for his mother to see. It involved lifting the left side of his lip and scrunching up the side of his face. The scowl deepened as the riots went on, week after week.

There were all sorts of discussions on the radio as representatives of those on the blanket protest began to talk about a hunger strike. Decriminalization, remission, segregation, intransigence, political status. The words spun around in the boy's head.

He thought that God must have been a sly and complicated bastard to give people different words for normal things.

There was a statue of the blessed Saint Martin de Porres that they kept on the mantelpiece. His mother liked it, she joked, because it looked like Al Jolson. She took it down from the shelf when the hunger strike began and the boy had asked her why but she didn't reply. He thought maybe it had something to do with music. She was singing in a bistro in the city center. When the riots were at their worst she would take him to the bistro and have him sit on a stool near the piano, where he did his homework. She sang from seven until ten. The restaurant was quiet and she bought him a lot of Cokes, sang love songs that had no politics to them. She had a beautiful voice and sometimes he thought it was made more beautiful by all the cigarettes she smoked. He would watch the customers as they whispered. They were conspiratorial. They didn't talk loud or address each other by the clue of their first names. They hunched over their plates. It seemed to the boy that even the food was under siege.

At the end of the evening she always sang a song about ferrying her love over the ocean, but the sea was too wide and she could not swim over and neither did she have wings to fly.

He and his mother took a taxi home each evening and he would watch her in the kitchen, staring at the back door, a teacup shaking in her hand, cigarette smoke curling up from the butt placed on the edge of the saucer.

In her nightdress she would practice moving through the dark of the house, beginning in the kitchen, then along the hallway, her eyes closed, touching the welcome mat with her toes, reaching out to check the bolt on the door, turning around, climbing the stairs without holding the banisters, still blind so she would learn the whole landscape of the house, along the landing, and into the bathroom, where she would take the duvet out from the airing cupboard. And then she would kneel down by the bath to run the water, all the time her eyes still shut tight, both taps fully opened. She would plunge the duvet into the water and finally she would carry the dripping mass down the stairs and lay it against the bottom of the door in case the street outside went up in flames.

Always that strange collaboration. Outside, the arc of color. Inside, the duvet soaking.

THE BOY TRIED to stake out a cell in the caravan, one window, one bed, a jug of water, a fluorescent light, a chair, a galvanized bucket for a chamber pot. He stayed in the space, not breaking its borders, hungry for three hours until she came home—her face flushed with drink, he thought—and she was carting groceries: sausages, eggs, cheese, black pudding, three fresh loaves of bread.

I got the job.

Did you hear any news?

Two nights a week, she said.

Any news, Mammy?

Isn't that great?

Mammy.

She sat down at the table and lit a cigarette and stared at the ash as it crumpled and flared. His first day he went to see the doctor, she said. They took his weight and his blood pressure and all that. Gave him a water cooler and some salt tablets and they put him in a cell on his own.

Salt tablets?

I think he must need them for—

Isn't salt a type of food?

I don't know, love. I don't think so.

How much water does he drink?

A few pints a day, I suppose.

How much weight has he lost?

Oh, God, I don't know, maybe a pound, love. Maybe more.

The boy pondered this for a while and then asked: Is he okay?

He's fine, I think. They put food by his bed though.

They what?

They put food in his cell just in case. Leave it by his bed. On a little tray they wheel in and out. I heard it's better food than they ever gave him before. And they count every last chip and pea.

Pigs, said the boy, and he was delighted when she didn't scold him.

Did Grandma visit? he asked.

There's no visits. There's a priest in the prison and he phones her at night and he tells her everything that's going on. And some others keep in touch with her, too. And there's notes, they write notes on pieces of cigarette paper and get them smuggled out.

Jesus, they must have wild wee handwriting.

She gave a little chuckle and finished off the last of her cigarette. He noticed that she was smoking them farther than ever before, dragging all the way down to the filter, burning all the white paper, and that her fingers were a darkening yellow.

Will he write me one?

You never know, but I'm sure he's exhausted.

Can we visit when there's visits?

We'll see.

A thought occurred to him and he asked: How much does he weigh?

She was startled and said: No idea, love.

Approximately?

I don't know, love. I haven't seen him in oh I don't know how many years. When your father and I got married, that was the last time, he was one of the ushers. All jazzed up in a suit and dickie bow and he looked good. But now, oh, I couldn't even guess.

Approximately, Mammy.

She scrunched her eyebrows: Ten and a half stone maybe, but you shouldn't be thinking about that, love, he's going to be all right, don't think that way, it's not good.

Why not?

Ah, come on, love.

Come on where?

Young man. Don't push it please . . .

You said come on.

I said enough.

Pardon me?

Enough! she shouted.

Enough what? he said gently.

She slammed her fist down on the table and there was silence.

He entered his space again and he lay on the thin yellow mattress and he put his arms behind his head, stared at the ceiling, imagined himself into his uncle's body, his knuckles tightening white around a bed frame, knives and forks banging against a heating pipe, the sound of boots along a metal catwalk, the taunts of screws, helicopters outside the window flying over the razor wire, candles winking at a vigil outside the gate, the light slowly dwindling, prayers being intoned, his stomach beginning the first of its small and poignant rumblings. A plate of cod appeared on the table beside him, with a slice of lemon and a big heaping of chips. An apple tart with ice cream. Packets of sugar for the tea. Milk in tiny little cartons. All carefully ranged by the bed for maximum temptation. A shout went up from a distant cell and other roars began to reverberate around the prison. Word went around that a screw was coming. Someone passed the boy a cigarette from a neighboring cell, spinning it across the floor on a length of fishing wire, stopping a few inches from the cell, so that he got on his knees and used a page from the Bible to drag the cigarette under the door frame. The rollie was just thin enough to fit under the door and he lay back and snapped it aflame—by striking the match off his thumbnail—and he brought the smoke down long and hard into his lungs, made rings in the air against the ceiling, but then his mother came and broke the borders of his cell and stood above his bed.

All right young man, she said. If you're good, I have a special treat for you.

She brought him out of his cell to the Formica table,

where she had prepared a full fry, which he pushed away at first but then he speared the sausages and broke the skin of the eggs and dunked the fresh bread and ate with an anger that gave him a stomachache. When he looked at his empty plate he imagined it full and then he threw his prison blanket across it and groaned and tried to stop the hunger pains and all the quiet, necessary shiverings.

RANGED IN A NOTEBOOK in parallel columns:

Day one	147 lbs	66.8 kg
Day two	146 lbs	66.36 kg
Day three	144.9 lbs	65.86 kg
Day four	143.9 lbs	65.4 kg

AT THE TABLE he looked at his meals, pushed the food around on his plate. Every day there was news of an impending reconciliation, but always the talks broke down and even the radio announcers sounded tired. The newspapers printed cartoons he didn't understand. He tried to read the editorials and the word *breakthrough* became ambiguous to him.

He was reminded of a winter thaw years ago in Derry

that had raised the rot of a neglected greyhound. When the sun began to shine the stench had risen.

He decided he would not take food. When his mother wasn't watching, he swept the chicken and rice off his plate and he stuck only to water. He lay back on his bed and tried to form a manifesto in his mind—he would not eat until all his uncle's demands were given in to: the right to wear his own clothes, to have parcels and visits, to have remission restored, to refrain from prison work, to have free association. He didn't understand all the demands but he whispered them aloud to the night anyway and fought the pangs in his stomach. He woke with his mouth dry.

At breakfast he took his cornflakes outside and dumped them in the long grass.

On his bed that afternoon he stretched out his torso and thought about how flat his belly was becoming. The boy looked for clues to his uncle's body in his own: the chest concave, the ribs taut, the arms bare and rippled. His mother caught him staring in the mirror but she said nothing. He left abruptly, wandered along the cliff face, and spent hours in an abandoned Vauxhall down near a cove. He sat at the steering wheel, faced the shattered windshield, and began driving home, down narrow country roads toward the city. The gear lever rattled in his fingers. The accelerator touched the floor and he was tremendously skillful with the clutch. He broke through roadblocks and avoided the pursuit of a black helicopter. A crowd of masked men waited for him on the side of the road. He picked them up and they traveled east toward the jail for their own breakthrough.

At dinnertime he asked if he could eat outside on his own, and when his mother agreed he walked out, feeling lightheaded, with a dull throb in his stomach now. He threw the plateful in the grass beside the morning's cornflakes, most of which had already been picked over by seagulls.

THE GIRL STOOD above the vat of oil, waiting for it to heat. She had a pretty face and he was embarrassed when she looked at him a second time. Outside the church bells struck eleven chimes. He had been on hunger strike for thirty-four hours now. A picture of the Italian football team was hung above the rack of sweets. A statue of a saint was taped to the cash register. His palms were sweaty and he switched the coins from hand to hand. You're the first customer of the morning, she said to him. He nodded and looked at his reflection in the stainless steel frontispiece of the counter. It made his face alternately fat and thin. He rose up and down on the tips of his toes and scrunched his face violently, then stopped when the girl behind the counter giggled.

When he finally came out of the chip shop he was weeping, the vinegar so pungent that afterward he could smell it on his hands for days.

Day Eight	140.1 lbs	63.68 kg
Day Nine	139.3 lbs	63.32 kg
Day Ten	138.6 lbs	63 even

THE KAYAK WAS OUT EARLY. He saw how the old couple plied gracefully through the water and right then he hated them for their solitary joy, for the tandem rhythm they struck, for the way they knew each other's moves in what he was sure was silence.

He felt like a lone sniper at dawn, looking down on them.

They were a hundred yards out, moving parallel to the headland. The waves rocked the boat up and down; it could have been the single beat of a cardiac machine. Farther out, there were whitecaps that broke early, but the kayak never moved off its course, the blades cutting the air, the nose sideways to the breakers. It was startlingly yellow on the water, as if the sea had decided to give it more color than it deserved and only the old couple, in their drab clothes, diluted that color, the man in a blue work shirt, the woman in a gray dress.

The boy said to himself: Bang. Bang.

On the step of the caravan his mother watched him out of the corner of her eye. He had been badly constipated after his hunger strike but he had not told her the reason why. She had given him medicine that had caused him to throw up, but now he told her that he felt much better, that he would like to take a walk into town.

She reached into the pocket of her jeans and dug deep and came up with a fifty-pence coin, which she handed to him.

Fifty pence?

Yeah.

What am I going to do with fifty pence?

Get in half the trouble you will with a pound.

The boy chuckled.

Fair enough, he said.

He ran down the hill, knocking at the brambles with a switch of stick. At the foot of the hill the chill of the early summer day cut through his shirt, and he hugged his arms around himself.

Out on the water the kayak had become a tiny speck.

In town there were some older teenagers at the back of an alley and he spied on them from the window of the video arcade. The light from a blue neon sign pulsed upon them. They too wore black drainpipes and white shirts, but their hair was shorter than his and they had sideburns. He smiled when he saw that they wore black armbands. He wanted to go outside and tell them that his uncle was on hunger strike—they would look at him with a certain awe and feel a shiver and know him to be a hard man. They would share their cigarettes and give him a nickname. He would show them his penknife and lie about how he once sliced a soldier from neck to stomach like a gutted deer.

One of the teenagers looked around furtively and the boy was startled to see him bring a bag of glue to his mouth.

The boy turned immediately and put his fifty pence into the machine. It lit up. He played with a bead of sweat beginning at his brow, but the teenagers in the alleyway kept their faces to the plastic bag. He wondered what it was like to get high. Back home he had never seen any of his friends taking drugs—once there had been a pusher in the house next door and she had ended up with bullets in both knees. He would listen to her coming along the street and her crutches struck the ground, a shrill metallic language. Late at night when she played her stereo he could hear the crutch tapping out a

rhythm against the floor, but when she kept dealing the vig-
ilantes kicked her door down, put two bullets in her elbows,
and two more in her ankles for good measure, after which
she disappeared altogether, and people said she'd gone to
England, where she was dealing from a wheelchair.

He stole another look at the alleyway.

They breathed the bag in and out and it looked to him
like the beat of a strange gray heart. Between hits of the
glue they smoked cigarettes and one of the youths noncha-
lantly left a lit cigarette behind his ear and the smoke curled
up above his head.

The boy patted his pockets and cursed himself for
spending all his money on one game, but he controlled the
machine for two hours until his fingers began to ache, and
when he looked again to the alleyway the youths were gone.
On the ground lay a ring of cigarette butts and a patch of
vomit. At the far end of the laneway was graffiti that said:
SMASH THE H-BLOCK. Beyond that were the words: BOBBY
SANDS M.P., R.I.P. He saluted the graffiti and wished he had
some spray paint so he could put his uncle's name in high
strong letters all around the town.

The sea threw waves on the beach, and out on the water
he spied some fishing boats. One of them flew a black flag
and the Irish tricolor promiscuously from atop its cabin.

The boy ran down to the water's edge and waved at the boat, but there was no response. He walked along the hard edge of the sand, whistling.

Good on ye, he said to the disappearing boat.

He took off his shoes and toyed with the water, daring it to wet his toes. The cold sand sucked around his feet and made gurgling noises. He found himself laughing and he wasn't quite sure if he should be enjoying himself or not, in this strange town, on this strange beach, in this strange loneliness.

He stepped in farther until the sea was up to his ankles and he kicked up spray and the droplets made shapes and parabolas in the air. Mathematics was the only thing he enjoyed in school, though he told nobody, and he wondered now if he could ever chart the arc of a droplet of water. It would be an odd graph, he thought, captured in a millisecond, from one end of an axis to another. He could create a formula for moving water and it would be decipherable only to him.

The sea no longer felt cold and in a moment he was running along the sand, kicking furiously and laughing, and the sea itself seemed doomed to the fact of his joy.

He shouted to the waves: Try me, come on, try me. He was soaked to the knees and moving at the edge of the

empty beach like some piebald horse with his feet in the air
and his neck outstretched, until he stopped quite suddenly
and felt his face flush.

On the pier sat three girls, dangling their legs over the
edge. They were whispering to each other some secret
which the boy knew was about him. He walked along the
beach with his head hung to his chest and then gave another
skip in the air just in case they were watching.

He climbed over the pier and, out of their view, he sat on
the rocks, took out a cigarette butt from his shirt pocket, and
began drying it in the sun.

As he waited he watched the girls move out onto the
sand, where they sat together and shared an ice-cream cone.
One of the girls stood up and took off her red pullover. She
had short blond hair and her breasts stood out against a white
shirt. When she placed her arms behind her head to stretch,
it gave him an erection. He disappeared behind a large rock
and, unzipping, he cradled the length of himself in his hand.
As he masturbated he watched the girl stretching farther,
furrowing a line in the sand with her toes. He locked his eyes
on the back of her body and, when she put her arms behind
her head and twisted once more, he cupped his other hand.
He closed his eyes and bit his lip and, when he was finished,
tucked his penis away, darting a look around.

The old couple were bringing the kayak in to the pier. They were bent to the work of paddling so they had not seen him, but still the boy felt ashamed as he wiped his palm on a nearby rock. He took a small stone and fired it so that it arced through the air and hit the water about ten yards from the kayak, landing gently, so that the old man turned, puzzled.

Go and shite, whispered the boy.

SHE WAS ON THE STEPS of the caravan staring into a small handheld mirror. She had a tube of lipstick to her mouth and she ran her tongue over her teeth. She seemed beautiful and he was angered by this and he wanted to tell her to wipe the lipstick off, but he knew she was just preparing for her gig. She would lean seductively into the microphone and sing about women tying up their hair with black velvet bands.

Mammy. I want to wear a black armband, he said, standing on the step.

Ah, don't start, not now, please. No.

Ach, why not?

Because I said no.

I want one.

Listen to your mother, please, and when I say no—

I saw some boys in town wearing them.

You don't need one.

I even saw some wee girls too.

He exaggerated the word and she lowered her head to the mirror, touched the glass with her forefinger, as if she would find the answer written there. No, she said, and in that one word her accent seemed now distinctly southern, as if she had changed the place of her birth.

The boy muttered beneath his breath and pushed past her into the caravan and then he saw the portable radio on the kitchen table wrapped in a blue ribbon.

His mother came to the doorway and stood mantled by light.

I didn't think you'd like to play chess on your own, she said. I thought I'd get you a little something. A present. For when I'm out working. You might be able to tune in a pirate station.

The boy lifted the radio and turned the dial and some scratchy music sounded out. He put it to his ear and began to sway.

When your father and I were young we were in Portrush for a holiday and the room had a radio and we used to listen to a station called Radio Luxembourg, she said. Sometimes the reception was bad and your father would pick up the radio and walk around the room and sometimes I thought the music was coming from him—

Did Daddy have a radio when he was young?

Sure, your daddy was the first man in Derry listening to the Rolling Stones.

They're the ones who sing *I Can't Get No Satisfaction*.

They are indeed.

What music did my uncle like?

I'm sure he liked the same things, she said, and then she hesitated a moment, looked at the boy, and added: I'm sure your uncle had a radio too.

Like this one?

Perhaps, who knows.

With an aerial and all?

Possibly. Maybe he listened to the same songs your daddy did. *Brown Sugar. Honky-Tonk Woman.* They were great days for music, you know.

Aye. Thanks, Mammy.

Do you like it?

I do, aye. It's dead on. I love it.

It's so you won't get lonely up here.

He turned the dial up and down, got mostly faint signals, except for one Gaelic radio station that came in loud and foreign.

He flicked his hair and then said: Mammy?

What, love?

I still want to wear a black armband, though.

She shook her head. You'd give the Pope heart problems, she said.

A thought occurred to him, and just as she stepped outside he asked her what was the count of his uncle's blood pressure.

I've no idea. Why would I know that?

Just curious.

You're a strange lad sometimes.

What's normal blood pressure?

Much too high when you're around. She laughed.

Seriously, Mammy.

One hundred and twenty over seventy, I think.

He imagined the way a line would slash between both figures.

She looked at her lipstick in the mirror once more: Enjoy your radio, she said. I'll be home by midnight. Don't forget to lock the door.

As she went away from the caravan he noticed she was wearing very tight pants. Her guitar case swung beside her. She had stickers from all over the country on the case, and he often thought it looked as if she was carrying an atlas:

Dublin, Belfast, Limerick, Cork plastered on the side. Her leather jacket too looked like it had been on a long journey. Years ago, she and his father had gone around the country in a Bedford van with three or four other musicians. His father had been the roadie and he had constructed special wooden platforms for the speakers to sit on. But the days of show bands were long over, and his father was years dead, killed in a traffic accident in Kildare when his car had skidded out of control after blowing a right front tire. The boy had been seven then. He tried to recall the funeral but couldn't; all that appeared were some shadowy figures with a box on their shoulders that he had later leaned across and kissed before it went into the back of the hearse.

He hugged the radio to himself and watched his mother go.

She was very careful to step to the side of the muddy path that twisted and curved away from the headland. Her feet left prints where she walked and the grass bent back as if it held the memory of her and all the places she had been.

When she was fully out of sight, the boy went to his duffel bag and took out an old black T-shirt. He tore a strip and fastened it high on his arm and it could have been a thick banded tattoo. It felt tight when he moved his arm into a muscle and he watched his reflection in the window for a moment.

You're looking well, man.

Ach, I'm all right.

You're right fit.

I am, aye.

You could kick the shite out of someone.

I could, aye.

A good beating. You're the man for it. That's for sure.

I am indeed.

He put the radio to his ear again and moved around the caravan within the space of his cell. To walk the perimeter took him just seven steps. He noticed that the reception was best at the window that looked out to sea and he stayed there, listening to a very dim signal from far away, a David Bowie number that he sang along with. There were radios in the prison, he had heard, small crystal sets. The parts were smuggled in and the prisoners tucked them away, hid them in their beards, their armpits, the crook of their elbows, even their arses. They reassembled them in their cells, and sometimes the best reception came when they put the crystal parts in their mouths and leaned close to the windows, so that their whole bodies became the news of what was happening to them.

The boy extended the aerial of his radio. He put it to his mouth. It made no difference to the sound.

He stood looking out to sea, the Bowie number fading now. The sun went very fast when it touched the horizon. The colors in the sky bled away. It became shadowy. Darkness doesn't fall, he thought as he swayed to the radio, it rises up from the bottom of the sea and begins to breathe around us.

| Day twelve | 136 lbs | 61.8 kg | 120/70 |
| Day thirteen | 135.2 | 61.45 | ? |

TWISTING IN HIS SLEEP, he turned his face to the wall in shame when she brought her sleeping bag over to his bed and nudged in beside him, saying she had heard him thrashing. She smelled of the bar—cigarette smoke in her hair and her voice hoarse from singing—and the boy wondered if she had enjoyed herself, and he hoped not, he couldn't bear the thought of her laughing.

He could feel the blood racing through the veins in his arm and furtively he loosened the tight strip of black cloth. She zipped herself into her own bag and touched his hair and she said: Everything will be all right.

The boy pushed himself in against the wall and bit his tongue.

It's a nice little pub, she said. Lots of tourists. They put a tip jar out for me and I made a few bob. It was one of those old jars like what you used to get bonbons in. I put a pound in the bottom first to make sure everyone put in paper money and nearly everyone did. Isn't that funny? We're going to like it here eventually, wait'll you see.

Did you hear anything more?

I caught the phone ringing earlier by the pier and it was your grandma calling us.

When are we going to get a real phone?

Oh, one of these days.

What did she say?

She said she loves you.

That's what she always says.

She said she wants for you to be strong.

Strong, he said, his voice breaking high and then deep, and he wondered to himself if he was two different people within just one word, both a boy and a man.

If you're on hunger strike, he asked, does your blood pressure go up or down?

You ask the strangest questions.

Well, he said. Up or down?

I've no idea, replied his mother. I imagine both the numbers fluctuate. Why d'you ask?

Ach, no reason really.

You're a mystery.

A good mystery?

Yes, a good mystery, she laughed.

I don't want to be a mystery.

Well then you're not.

Ach, Mammy, he said, and he turned himself to the wall.

He heard her body swish and move within the sleeping bag, trying to get comfortable. He was surprised when he found himself awake in the morning, alarmed that he had managed to fall asleep, his mother beside him, gently wheezing.

ON THE BEACH there stood a pole. A red-and-white life preserver ring hung from it. He went there late in the evening while his mother was gone, singing in the pub.

The beach was deserted. Windblown litter moved along the sand. A bright light burned in the house of the old kayaking couple, and the boy imagined that it was the safe house. He waved to his comrades and took to firing stones at the beach pole. At first he missed with most of his shots, but more and more the stones began to make small dents in the wood. He developed rhythms of firing and the pole became a soldier in riot gear. The life-preserver ring was his shield. The soldier had a baby face and spoke with a London accent. The boy stood back and threw a rock, which hit the eyes of the pole, and the soldier squealed. Some blood came from the eyebrow and the boy danced and spun in the sand and executed a perfect kung-fu kick in the air. He fired another stone, aiming this time at the neck. The boy had heard once that this is where military gear was most exposed.

In the house back north he had never been allowed out at night, but now he began his own riot on the sand.

Fuck you, he shouted.

The soldier crouched down at the knee but still the rock caught him and sent him reeling backward as sirens wailed and Molotov cocktails were carried in from the sea. The boy tore off his T-shirt and wrapped it around his face to act as a sort of balaclava. He ran forward and spat at the pole, and when he turned the soldier tried to hit him from behind, but the boy ducked with perfect timing. He swung around and kicked the soldier in the face and blood erupted from his nose.

You'd try it, would you? Come on. Get up. Come on.

In the distance he heard the familiar drone of Saracens.

He went and put his thumb to the neck of the soldier from London. He said: Call your boys off or I'll kill you. He pressed his finger harder into the neck. The soldier nodded meekly and the vehicles retreated.

He began to comb the beach for stones that fitted his hand, and he developed a tremendous accuracy with the rocks, cutting the air smoothly.

The tide was low and he took up different positions on the beach, hammering the stones against the pole, which became three soldiers, all standing in one another's shadows. He dodged their rubber bullets and he taunted them from the rooftops.

Try me, youse fuckers.

At the end of his evening's rioting, he walked up to the pole and smiled and told the soldiers that a man had to do what a man had to do. They were nothing but stupid wankers, he said, didn't they know that? The soldiers whimpered in their incredible pain and one of them burned slowly from the feet up. The boy spat down and extinguished the fire and, with great humanity, allowed the soldier to live.

Seventeen	134.6 lbs	61.18 kg	110/68

• • •

ONE NIGHT HE STAYED by the sea until almost mid-night, when he saw his mother walking back down from the pub, carrying her guitar, and her shadow disturbed the globes of lamplight and then the darkness took her.

She was taking the long road, so the boy ran the short path up the hillside and was at the caravan before her.

His mother did not bring her sleeping bag over to lie beside him this time, but she came to his bed, kissed his hair, told him she loved him, took him in her arms and he was embarrassed by the weight of her hug. He wanted there to be a smell of drink on her, or some such violation, so he could pull away, but there wasn't.

It was the twenty-first day and she told him his uncle had lost seventeen pounds and that the food was still kept at the bottom of the bed like an equinox between life and death. He was still in the cell block but might soon be removed to the prison hospital. It was said that his spirits were good, although a cough was tearing at his chest and he found it hard to swallow water. He was reading books for the first time in years, poetry and a play by W. B. Yeats. When he opened the Perspex window of his cell he could hear the Orangemen outside the prison gates, playing their Lambeg drums, and it was like a slow torture to him.

She gave the boy a newspaper and he was surprised to remember that other people had lives too. An elderly woman had been killed by a soldier who thought the umbrella she carried was a rifle. A young father was shot coming out of a maternity ward. A tightrope walker from France had been set on fire as he tried to walk a rope between two housing estates in Derry—a Molotov cocktail had hit against his knee and he had continued walking as the flames rose high around him, dropping finally into the Foyle, his balance pole lost in the dark waters below him. On the streets, the rioting was worse than ever before: burning barricades, tear gas, rubber bullets, checkpoints.

There was still no news of a breakthrough, although some international committees were involved now too; everyone was clamoring for a solution, it had to come soon, it was inevitable.

His mother said she wondered sometimes if everyone had dropped small pieces of their sanity here and there, lost them so that the whole world had gone mad and things had fallen asunder.

How long was the longest hunger strike? he asked.

Sixty-something days.

And the shortest?

Oh, please, Kevin, let's not talk anymore about it.

It was forty days or so, wasn't it?

Just go to bed. Please, son. Please.

I'm just asking you.

And I'm just asking you, go on to bed, please.

He couldn't sleep, rose from his bed at four, tiptoed across the caravan, stole eighteen pounds from his mother's handbag, and went down to the town, avoiding the graveyard. The streets were quiet and eerie. The stars swung in their sockets above him. Bats harried the streetlamps. He fired stones at each of the three traffic lights in town and smashed the amber glass of one, found himself sprinting through the streets with imaginary policemen following.

Dawn broke over the mountains and light gnawed the town into shape.

He walked along the coast road until he managed to hitch a lift in a farmer's pickup truck. He sat sullen in the seat as the farmer talked about silage. The farmer said that the price of silage was in serious danger of bringing the government of Ireland to its knees. Silage was an issue they couldn't ignore. Silage was what would get them votes in this part of the world. The farmer had a deep smell of drink to him. He crunched through the gears. Once he put his hand on the boy's knee and said that in the north silage was a proper issue, even the Unionists were up in arms about it.

The boy sat on the edge of the seat and kept his hand on the door handle, just in case, until he was dropped off in the city center.

Thanks, he said to the farmer, and under his breath he muttered: Ye humpy cunt.

The city was in full throat. Tour buses negotiated corners. Cars careened around him. Music belched from record shops. On telegraph poles there hung signs that said: SUPPORT THE HUNGER STRIKERS! and from a balcony on Dominick Street black flags fluttered. The boy punched his fist in the air. Girls wore very tight jeans and he could see their nipples through the cloth of their T-shirts. You've got your high beams on, he whispered. He bent himself over at the waist to calm his erection. Down along by an archway he sang a little to a stray dog.

I'm going to get screwed and you're not.

Diddly-di-idle-day.

You're a dog and I'm a man.

Diddly-di-idle-day.

At the bus station he bought a ticket and played video games until he heard the bus announced over the tannoy. He boarded with a swagger, still singing his song.

When the bus driver mentioned over the microphone about a connection to Derry City from Donegal, the boy punched his fist in the air once more and said: Brits Out, Me In.

Just half an hour into the trip two policemen boarded the bus. They told the driver they were looking for a dark-eyed runaway who has bought a ticket from Galway all the way to Northern Ireland. He slid down in the rear seat, but a policeman touched his shoulder, leaned down, and said his name aloud. He began to cry. Your mammy's worried sick, they said. They were gentle as they guided him down along through the seats, other passengers staring at him.

He asked the police to turn on the squad card siren as they drove out from the city of Galway along the coast road, and they did, and he sat in the back seat, grinning, careful the policemen wouldn't see him.

Twenty-four	128.9 lbs	58.59 kg	110/65	Removed to the prison hospital.

SHE STAYED HOME with him now in the evenings and she wrote songs in a notebook. He had taken a peek at the book and noticed that she had written his father's name

in curly letters with a love heart ringed around
schoolgirl.

The songs were mostly about love and he noticed that
she liked to use the word *ocean* a lot in the lyrics. An ocean
of this and an ocean of that. Late each night the boy could
hear her humming tunes to herself when she thought he was
asleep.

He had promised her he would never run away again and
so, toward the end of the week, she took the gig in the pub
again. It was their only money, she told him, and she needed
to be able to trust him. He swore once more that he would
never leave no matter what. In the caravan he searched for
stations on the radio, sang along to a few, got bored, found
himself imagining beautiful women calling at the door. On
his bed he masturbated and cleaned the mess up with tissues.
He was careful that she wouldn't notice the tissues in the rub-
bish bin. After a few days he began sneaking down
to the town, stood on the rim of gray kegs at the back of the
bar, watching her. She sang with her eyes closed and her
lips very close to the microphone, holding the guitar close,
her foot tapping in time to the songs. The small crowd
seemed to sit under hats of cigarette smoke and the boy
willed them to give her a longer, louder round of applause,
to drop pound notes instead of coins into the tip jar.

At the end of the song called *Carrickfergus,* a young man blew his mother a kiss and the boy thought he should go into the bar and kick the fucker's teeth in, but instead he turned around and snarled at an old Alsatian that was tied up at the back of the pub. It kept its muzzle flat to the ground and, when the boy threw a rock, it rose surly and mistrustful and loped away to the farthest end of its chain.

Twenty-seven	127.3 lbs	57.8 kg	110/60	
Twenty-eight	126.8 lbs	57.6 kg	115/68	
Twenty-nine	126.3 lbs	57.3 kg	110/59	Tonight the fuckers put enough food out to feed an army.
Thirty	125.9 lbs	57.2 kg	105/65	

THE WEATHER BRIGHTENED and there were games on the beach. An odd bouquet of swimming togs and bikinis. Two women with skirts held high trod the low depths of the water as skeins of light caught the breaking waves. A small child threw a colored ball in the air. The ice-cream truck played its tinny tunes. The caps of swimmers bobbed on the sea and, farther out, an oil tanker seemed nailed down on the horizon.

His mother had bought him a pair of black shorts but he had refused them and now he felt the stickiness at the back of his trousers. He longed to take them off, but he stood with nonchalance at the rear of the beach while inwardly he cursed himself. He rolled up the sleeves of his shirt and noticed the line below which his arms were sunburned.

The sun climbed and shortened his shadow. He wondered if he threw himself down onto the sand would his shadow stand and watch him?

On the beach he saw the blond girl. She wore a red swimsuit this time and held a small radio to her ear. He watched her for half an hour, motionless in the sand, then he walked near the water. He was acutely conscious of his shoes and finally he took them off and strung them together, tucking his socks inside, and put them around his neck. The sand sucked his toes. The girl didn't look up at him at all. She had a forearm shading her eyes and he thought that if he had money he would buy her some sunglasses. He would walk up and give them to her and then sit beside her. They would get bronzed in silence. Soon they would kiss.

He began to jog along the beach, looking over his shoulder at her, turning at the far seawall, climbing the steps and circling around once more. He thought about trying to phone his grandmother, but his mother had always done the dialing and he didn't know the number.

A fresh breeze herded litter along the street and he walked past the alleyway where the older teenagers were breathing in their glue. They called after him and he hurried away, giving them two fingers from beneath his jacket.

Try me, he said under his breath.

You'd try me, would you?

Come on, so.

I'll kick the living shite out of ye.

He found himself suddenly outside the house of the old couple. It was a whitewashed bungalow and there were roses in bloom on the front driveway. It looked old, as if it had been sunk back into another decade, battered by years of the sea. The window frames were rotted. Some slates were missing from the roof. The gate, when he touched it, shivered. He hesitated and then opened the latch and turned around again. He went to the pier, sat with his back to a pierside bollard and smoked a cigarette, then raised the courage and walked nervously up the path. The old man answered the door.

Can I borrow the kayak?

Excuse me?

If I keep it close to shore?

The old man smiled and said: Wait please.

The boy was surprised that the man had a foreign accent. He couldn't place it and, for a moment, he was horrified that the old man might be English, but the accent didn't have any of those tones. English people, he thought, delivered their words on silver tongs. They spoke as if each word were being served with scones and china cups. Or else they spoke like soldiers, rolling the words around with menace and fear. This accent was different. It sounded like there was gravel in it. Like there were stones in the old man's larynx.

The old man shuffled out from behind the house carrying a life jacket with him and he beckoned the boy to come around the corner where the kayak was propped against the wall. The boy knew from watching that he would have to carry the kayak high above his head, and the old man nodded approval at the way he balanced the paddles on either shoulder. They negotiated their way through the rosebushes.

It's light, said the boy, although the boat was much heavier than he expected.

They went toward the sea and the man looked like he was walking toward days that once had been.

At the pier it took them a long time to adjust the spray skirt that would stop water from coming into the boat, and

an passed forward the single life jacket and told
boy to strap it on.

The boy looked toward the beach at the blond girl in
her swimsuit and felt a flush of embarrassment in his cheeks.

I don't need a life jacket.

Put it on.

Why?

The old man smiled, and with that the boy strapped on
the jacket.

I can swim you know.

I didn't ask you if you could or not.

Fair enough, said the boy.

It was high tide and there was no need to drop the boat
with ropes. They let it rest on the water and the old man
climbed down a couple of rungs and went into it with skill.
He said that dropping the boat from the pier was dangerous.
It was really just the lazy man's way out, he didn't like carrying the boat all the way around to the beach. The boy was
shocked at how difficult it was to get in—the old man
gripped his arm and guided him down, but still he was sure
he was about to fall. He could feel the sweat at his armpits
and he was suddenly happy for the life jacket. He put his
hands in the water and it felt remarkably cold.

The old man asked him if he was ready, but before the

boy could answer the boat was already gliding out into the water.

The sun lit up half the harbor and the rest was left in cloud shadow.

They said very little as they paddled around near the pier. The boy, at the front of the kayak, couldn't see the old man's face and he wondered if he was bored. The boat seemed fragile; the boy felt as if he was sitting on the very surface of the water and the nervousness made his fingers tremble. The paddle was hard to maneuver and, even in the calm waters of the harbor, he felt sure the kayak would tumble. They paddled farther out than any of the swimmers, and he felt as if the whole beach was watching them. His head felt light and airy and he had to fight the happiness. The old man showed him how to slice the paddle through the air, turning it in midswing so that it cut sideways, smooth and controlled. He said that all good things were done with economy. The blade should never go too deep into the water or else too much energy would be used. And there should never be too much of a splash when the paddle came out—it should look as if the sea had hardly been disturbed.

Don't fight the water, the old man said. Let the sea do the work.

The boy tried to place his accent, still uncertain, but after a while he grew comfortable with the paddling and asked where the old man was from.

Lithuania, he said.

Lithuania?

Do you know where that is?

I do, aye.

But the boy knew nothing of Lithuania, and when he finally admitted it they stopped by a buoy, steadied themselves, and the boy half turned his body around in the kayak. The old man drew a map of the USSR on the buoy with a wet finger, the borders gradually dissolving in the heat. There were large liver spots on the man's hand and the boy thought he could have made the map from them. The man said that he had once been a logger in pine forests near the Polish border, that he had been away from his country for over thirty years now, living in different parts of Europe, surviving on money from a relative in New York.

The boy felt dizzy in the vast geography that was contained in the harbor.

He learned that afternoon how to ply the paddle with a gentle twist so that the blade struck the water fully, how to curve the boat with a flick of his wrist. His arms grew tired and his knees ached from where they were bent in the well of the boat. When they pulled in to the pier the old man slapped him on the shoulder, said: You did well. Come back tomorrow. You'll learn more.

The boy ran home.

His mother was waiting for him and in the early evening, after dinner, she told him about his uncle, the reports that had come through on the pierside phone, and he imagined it: the pulse weakening, the feel colder, the taste of water metallic, the headaches, the dizziness, then the searing agony settling down to its own dullness, the eyes more shrunken every day, a dip in the blood pressure, a dribble cup at his head, bile on the pillow.

He'll go to the end, his mother said.

He'll die?

He'll go to the end, she said again.

Does he still have a cough?

He does, yeah.

And do they give him medicine?

No, there's sugars or proteins or something in the medicine, he can't take it.

Do they still keep food at his bed?

They do, yeah.

They're bastards, he said.

She hesitated at the curse, a reply quivering on her lips,

but she said nothing. Afterward she went down on her knees to pray.

Bastards, he whispered again before he went to sleep. He heard the muffled weeping from where she knelt.

THE OLD MAN was waiting for him on the low wall outside the house, rolling a cigarette with patience, sprinkling the tobacco evenly on the paper. The bones on the back of his hands were prominent, leading like a scallop to his fingers. He brought the cigarette to his lips and licked the paper and sealed it slowly. The boy had his own cigarette butts in his pocket that he had rescued from his mother's ashtray but he didn't want to light up in front of the old man. He watched with jealousy as the cigarette crisped and flared. Two thin streams of smoke came from the old man's nostrils and the boy leaned closer to get the smell of the tobacco.

Einam, said the old man.

Pardon me?

Let's go.

Shall I put on the spray guard?

The old man laughed and said: Skirt. I told you yesterday. It's called a skirt.

Shall I put it on?

Yes.

The boy looked behind his shoulder, pulled the spray skirt over his head and then lifted the kayak.

Instead of dropping the boat from the pier they went to the beach, kicked off their shoes and socks, and waded into shallow water. A drizzle had begun and the beach was empty. The boy got into the kayak and the old man stood waist-deep in the water beside him. He showed the boy how to right the boat if it ever overturned, by tucking his head in toward the boat, swishing out the paddle underwater, and snapping his hip upward, thereby rolling the boat right side up. It was very difficult, he said, with a double boat, but it was good to practice. If the worst came to the worst, the old man said, he could simply remove the spray skirt and hold on to the floating boat and hope the tide would carry him in.

Suddenly the old man tipped the boat and the boy went over in the water. He flailed around a moment and tried to bring his paddle up, but couldn't. The boy yanked the front of the spray skirt, and for a moment he was all commotion underwater and then he rose, spluttering and spewing. The old man leaned down and grabbed the boy under the armpits.

For fuck sake.

Pardon me?

Why did you do that?

Get in the boat.

I can't. Fuck sake. I'm soaking.

Get in, said the old man. I'll hold it.

Fuck sake.

He coughed up some seawater and spat it out and exaggerated his shiver.

Get in, said the old man, as he patiently tilted the boat in the air and dumped most of the water out. He did it with ease and then he steadied the boat and the boy climbed in again. He had to throw his leg over the side of the boat, making him feel vulnerable and stupid. His trousers were soaked and heavy. He felt the old man's hand on the small of his back and he wriggled away from the touch. When he finally got into the boat, his bare feet touched the water that was still in the well.

I'm fucking freezing.

The old man said nothing.

This is stupid.

It took an age to get the spray skirt adjusted once more and immediately the old man tipped the boat a second time.

The boy didn't even try to right the kayak with his paddle. He ripped at the spray skirt and came up spluttering once more. He stared at the old man, pushed the boat away, and threw the paddle after it. He was about to take the spray skirt off when the old man started laughing. The boy watched. The old man's head was thrown back in the air and his mouth was open and his eyes were closed.

What're you laughing at?

I'm laughing because it's funny.

I'd like to see you get dumped.

Would you?

Aye.

Would you really?

I would, aye.

The old man dropped himself backward in the water and he was submerged for a second and his cap floated on the surface. The boy reached for the cap and handed it to him when he came back up. Both of them began chuckling and the boy thought that they must have been a curious sight, out in the shallows of the sea, he and an old man, dripping wet, laughing.

After a while the old man clasped his side and breathed heavily and shook his head back and forth, then put his hand on the boy's shoulder, gave one final snortle, and said: Get in the boat.

Fair enough.

This time, he said, swish the paddle out properly.

Okay.

And no bad language please.

EACH DAY THEY WENT OUT in the boat as his uncle weakened farther. The town seemed small from the water, tucked down in the hollow between the headlands, fringed by the beach. In the distance the mountains contorted the blacktop roads to their liking. Beyond the mountains, the sky was cool and azure and serene. The whole scene, thought the boy, could have been taken for a postcard.

He and the old man remained in the harbor, going from buoy to buoy, sometimes nudging up against large boats, learning how to maneuver the kayak, guiding it in circles, making figures of eight, once or twice riding the waves in toward shore.

Birds pinwheeled above them and sometimes the old man pretended to talk to them, sounding curious caws and screeches that made the boy chuckle.

At lunchtime the old woman came out to the pier to watch, bringing them sandwiches and milk. They ate together on the pier, legs dangling over the water. He discovered that their names were Vytis and Rasa. When they spoke it was mostly in Lithuanian but the boy didn't mind;

he felt as if he were in another country anyway, and after a while he began to recognize certain words that came up constantly between them—*berniukas, duoshele, miela, pietus*—although he wasn't quite sure what they meant. After lunch they took to the boat again for an hour or so. The old man didn't wear a watch but he said he could tell the time from the local church bells, and he sometimes even anticipated their toll. He said he liked to be home early and that the finest thing about life was an afternoon nap, it was his favorite moment of the day, to draw the curtains and drift away into odd dreams.

While the old couple slept, the boy would hose down the kayak and then make his way back toward the caravan. He often dipped into the town's dustbins to find a newspaper and he checked the horoscopes—one afternoon he decided that his uncle's birthday must have fallen in Scorpio, since the newspaper said that there was difficulty now, but with a planet about to enter the sphere, all would suddenly become calm.

His mother was delighted by his kayaking and she said if he kept it up she would increase his pocket money, so that one day he might be able to buy his own boat. He took the extra money and immediately ran back down to town and spent it all in the video arcade.

On the fourth morning, he and the old man went beyond the harbor, careful when crossing the meeting of currents, out into the moving corduroy of sea waves.

The boy was excited by the distance that was put between him and the town. He cawed at birds in the air. Farther out, the horizon seemed vast and flattened by a pale blue sky. They paddled for an hour with their backs to the town, and the sea remained calm.

While they were floating, the boy half turned his body in the kayak. I want to tell you something, he said. You see this here black armband?

Yes?

He stuttered and found his throat going dry. Eventually he told the old man all about his uncle, and they paddled for an hour without saying another word.

He felt as if the whole harbor was weighted down with implication, that each splash of the water had a meaning, and as the silence took on a greater weight he thought that the Lithuanian would have something wise to say but as they brought the kayak in toward the pier the old man simply cleared his throat and lowered his voice and said that he was sorry, that it was a sad story, that he too had been unhappy as a boy for a reason that no longer mattered, that his joy now was in simple things that needed no memory.

| Thirty-five | 123.4 lbs | 56.09 kg | 105/55 |
| Thirty-six | 122.9 | 55.86 kg | 107/52 |

AT MASS HE WAS SURPRISED that some older people recognized her from when she was a girl. They smiled and declared she looked like a teenager, which made him shiver with embarrassment. He created a gulf between them by putting the hymnal on the seat. His mother had made him wear a clean blue shirt with a button-down collar, and on purpose he let the tail of it hang out from his trousers. During the sermon she tried to tuck it in but he pushed her hand away and she just smiled at him.

The church was new and high-windowed and antiseptic.

When they went for Communion he walked a few steps behind her. For the first time he properly heard the words: This is the body of Christ. He wondered if the hunger strikers who had already died had taken the last rites and, if they had, did they receive bread before they died? He found himself tortured by the question and he had visions of emaciated men walking around the prison hospital with single patches of white on their tongues wondering whether they should swallow or not. The weight of the bread held their tongues down and so they could not ask the question of God. Their eyes watered. Slowly the bread dissolved on their tongues and entered their saliva and the hunger strike was broken. A prison doctor came and gloated. The men sank to their knees and died from starvation anyway.

He felt his mother elbowing him in the ribs and he looked up to see that the Mass had ended.

Outside, the priest was shaking hands with the congregation. The boy waited on a distant stone wall while his mother made her way through the crowd. He noticed that the priest brushed his hand against his mother's elbow and the boy said aloud: You horny bastard.

They were given a lift to town by a man with a long and sunburned face who asked if they were going to the pony races. His mother said no with a firmness that delighted the boy.

In the newsagent's they bought the Sunday newspapers and two loaves and four cream eclairs. As they were emerging from the shop, he saw the old couple entering. They looked as if they'd been toiling in their garden.

The old woman winked at him and the man patted him on the head and the boy could feel the delicate weight of the old man's hand as he walked away from the shop.

That's my friend, he said to his mother.

Oh, that's him? He's not exactly a bed of roses, s̶ with a chuckle.

What's that supposed to mean?

I'm just kidding.

What's it mean?

I'm joking, love.

You smell too. You smell worse than he does, you know that?

Listen, I'm just kidding you, love. Take it easy.

He scowled and found himself trying to sniff at his own armpits as he slouched behind her. He remembered his chess pieces, and as he followed his mother he thought to himself: Fuck the queen, I'm a knight.

In the caravan they spread out the Sunday papers on the table. There were photographs of his uncle from years ago. He ran his fingers over the face, then cut the pictures out very carefully. He put one of them in his shirt pocket and taped the other above his bed. Later, as he played chess with his mother, using the wooden pieces, he patted the photo in his pocket and it seemed as if his fingers were moving over his uncle's ribs. They felt prominent, like the ribs of a hungry horse. The bones made a sound like some musical instrument, and when he shoved his fingers deeper into the pocket he could feel the water swish in his uncle's belly.

• • •

IN THE GRAVEYARD after kayaking he found another pint glass at the site of the young man. This one had no lipstick, but it was ribbed with beer stains, perfect circles from where each gulp had been taken. He took the glass home and she inadvertently cleaned it and put flowers in it and placed it on the table, neatly positioned between the salt and pepper shakers, the flowers nodding in the wind every time the door of the caravan opened. After a while he began to like the idea of the glass being used, and he wondered if, by the end of the summer, he would have a little collection. A neighbor in their housing estate had kept rubber bullets, divining their histories from their scars—what wall they smashed into, what car, what warehouse, what flesh. The deeper the scar, the shorter the distance the bullet had flown. It was a simple logic the boy might apply to the residue of rings that were left on the side of the pint glass.

Thirty-eight	121.8	55.3	
Thirty-nine	121.4 lbs	55.1	
Forty	121 lbs	54.9	That's the amount of time Jesus went without food.
Forty-one	120.6 lbs	54.8 kg	

• • •

IN THE CARAVAN MIRROR it seemed to him that he looked older now and he found a single hair on his chest. In the morning he went toward town with a sort of brazenness and his shirt ambitiously undone.

At the end of the pier he blew kisses to the women who wore the skimpiest bikinis. They gestured back and invited him to their bedrooms and they made love endlessly, sometimes two or three of them all at once—they liked the way he talked and they told him he had the biggest willy they'd ever seen. He chuckled and whooped along the beach-front road, hearing them shout that it was massive, absolutely massive, their husbands together couldn't find a penis that size if they strung them end to end. When the old man came out of his house and asked him what he had been screaming about, the boy blanched and stuttered and said it didn't really matter, he was just shouting at the fishing boats, and the old man told him that was as good an occupation as any. When he was far enough away from the house the boy began laughing once more and the women called his name from all angles.

SHE CAUGHT HIM late one evening sitting on the grave-yard wall, smoke rings curling up above his head. She checked through her handbag and told him not to steal any more cigarettes. He lied and told her he would quit.

Your daddy never smoked, she said.

They sat on the cliff, under an inkening sky, and the boy was surprised to see her cry although she said it was the wind that disturbed her eyes. She said she remembered a time before she and his father got married. It was the sixties and they would come down from the north to camp for the weekend in an abandoned wooden hut by the seaside not so far from this town. At night in the old hut they would cuddle. She said this with a wink and the boy laughed with her. Cuddle, she said again. Cuddle. His mother was up on her feet now and animated with memory. There were fishermen in that town, she told him, and often the birds came and plucked whatever fish innards were left near the boats. The birds would fly to the roof of the hut and sometimes drop the leftovers there so the roof had begun to sag and rot, and once a beam fell. The air was sweet and hushed during those summers, and when autumn came, leaves blew in on top of them. They stayed in the hut, his mother and father, cuddling.

His father's face rose up in his mind, long wispy hair going bald, dark eyes, an abrupt nose. He thought he could reach out and touch him.

She was laughing now as she talked and she seemed suddenly very young to him, but after a while he mentioned his uncle and they felt instantly guilty about their laughter.

Tell me about him, he said.

I never really knew him.

Did Daddy like him?

When they were young, yeah. They worked on the farm together. They had good times. They brought in the hay and milked the cows and mended walls when they needed mending. She paused: When they were older they argued.

What about?

Your father never believed that the cure for war was war.

See, said the boy, even you say it's a war.

She ran a ringlet of hair around her finger: It's a war, yes, it's a war, she said sadly.

Then they should get what they want.

They should, yeah, maybe.

It's simple.

Nothing's simple, love.

Do you hate him?

Of course I don't hate him. He's my brother-in-law.

I know you hate him. I can tell. You hate him. I know.

Ah, love.

He was set up.

Come on now, let's—

Eighteen years for explosives he never used, the boy said.

That's maybe not all he did.

It's all he got charged for. Explosives.

That's true, but you never know—

I do know. He was set up.

I don't like it any more than you do. But others are dying too. Innocent ones.

He didn't even have a proper trial.

Neither did the ones who died, she said.

The boy thought about this and then said: Why can't we go home, Mammy?

I thought you liked it here now? With the kayaking and all? I thought you were getting settled in?

The waves pounded on the cliff face below them and the boy plucked at a spear of grass, put it between his teeth. He watched as a shooting star fishtailed in the sky above him.

Why can't we go home? he asked again.

She sighed: Because I don't want to be there to see it.

Well, I do.

I don't want for you to see it, love.

I'm not a child, he said.

They sat in silence until he asked her if his father had ever done anything bad in his life and she said: No, never, and he knew by the way she said it that she was telling the truth.

ONE SPECIFIC MEMORY of his father came back to him: The boy was just five years old. Some tinkers came to the door to sell a fridge. His father was between jobs, they had little money, and there was no fridge in the house. Milk went sour, leftovers grew mold. His parents had often talked about buying a fridge and this one was being sold for next to nothing, twenty pounds. The boy was excited at the thought of cold milk.

His father stepped outside the door to examine the fridge, but when he found the scorch marks on the side paneling he simply turned and said No, and closed the door on the travellers. Bomb-damaged, said his father to his mother.

Forty-four	119.4	54.27	105/60
Forty-fi			

IT'S OVER, she shouted as she ran up the hillside, it's over, it's over, it's over. He threw his notebook in the air and ran out from the caravan. She was thumping the air with her fist. Her cheeks were flushed with color. He hugged her and

m around and each of them fell to the ground
their shoes off and sent them cartwheeling
through the air. Breathless they lay there in the long grass
and she said that the prisoners had released a statement, all
was agreed, there were only a couple of formalities left. She
stood up and danced on the orange gas cylinder at the back
of the caravan. I knew it would finish! she shouted. Thank
you, God!

He took her hand and she jumped down from the cylinder and they ran through the grass to the cliffs, where she
was panting so hard that she swore she would give up cigarettes forever. They danced way above the sea, twirling and
high-stepping. Later, for dinner, she cooked up a huge meal
of sausages, rashers, tomato, eggs, and fried bread and they
had red lemonade floats for dessert. The ice cream left a rim
of white mustache above her lip and he showed it to her in
the mirror and she cackled with joy. She broke out a bottle
of wine and even allowed him one puff at the very end of
her cigarette. He pretended it made him very dizzy and he
staggered around the caravan.

Watch this! he roared. Watch this! They turned the radio
up very loud and they stepped outside, took hold of each
other's elbows, and began to spin, and for a moment everything seemed minutely perfect.

• • •

LATER THAT NIGHT—after the radio announced another breakdown in the talks—he unzipped his sleeping bag and shimmied his way down to the end of the bed, making sure he didn't expose himself through the gap in his pajamas. At the foot of the bed he pulled on his father's white shirt and, over that, a fisherman's sweater to keep himself warm.

He filled a saucepan with water, grabbed a loaf of bread from the rack above the stove, and went and sat at the kitchen table. Slowly he tore the crusts from all the slices and arranged them like a fence around the table. He placed the radio in the center of the crusts.

His mother was watching him from across the caravan. Her eyes were red from crying once again.

The only light was that of the moon, which had leaped to the lintel of the window.

He wet the bread and then squeezed it into the approximation of a cylinder. He massaged it gently with his fingers and then pressed tight where the neck should be. The bread gave nicely. It seemed to accept the whim of his hands.

He fanned his fingers down the length of the cylinder and dented the bread with his knife to give it a ribbed appearance at its foot. The blade pressed into the soft bread.

He straightened out the bottom so it would stand on its own on the table. Bending down to eye level with the piece, he gave it a crown and a set of eyes that looked out at him crookedly. He smoothed out the remaining thumbprints and then took a pen and tried to fill the eyes in with ink, but the bread wouldn't take the ink. He thought for a moment and went to the cupboard and found a tin of cocoa. Mixing the cocoa with water, he made a paste.

He put the tine of a fork into the paste and dropped a tiny amount where the eye should be. The brown dye seeped into the bread. The eye looked to him like it was bruised from a fight.

What's that?

It's the queen.

She sat up in her sleeping bag: It looks real.

He put it in the palm of his hand and rolled it along his fingertips. The piece had taken him an hour to make and there was a marvelous precision to it, most of all he liked the ribbed bottom. He sat at the table, thinking of his uncle, wondering if it was a suicide and if that was a mortal sin. Yet allowing a man to die would be a mortal sin too, surely? His head spun and his throat felt dry. He continued to roll the chess piece from finger to finger. Under his breath he cursed his uncle's stupidity and wished he would hurry up and eat something, and then hated himself for the thought of these things.

His mother was still watching him intently, so he stabbed the queen in the eyes with the prong of the fork and when her eyes were hollowed out began destroying the crown. Then he held the chess piece high in the air and licked his lips and then, with great theater, he ate it with a smile and a sort of savagery.

That's what I think of the Queen, he said.

He chewed while staring at his mother, then picked the bread from between his teeth. It had tasted soggy and awful. His mother propped herself up with her head on her hand and her neck seemed to loll sideways.

Don't be so angry, please, she said.

He went to the bin and spit the last of the bread out: I'll be angry all I want to; it's my life!

Please don't.

They're allowing him to die.

Maybe he's choosing to die, love.

It's the same thing.

Come here and get some sleep.

I don't want to sleep.

The bogeyman will get you.

Mammy, he said, I'm thirteen. Bogeyman. Christ!

She fidgeted with the zip on her sleeping bag and she put her head to her pillow and watched him as he spread his hand wide on the table and began to stab the empty spaces between his fingers. The knife made a high sound against the Formica.

Don't ruin the table.

I won't.

Why don't you put the knife away?

He snapped the blade shut.

Fuck the Queen! he shouted suddenly, and he startled himself with the curse. Fuck Maggie Thatcher! Fuck them all! Fucking cunts! Fuck every soldier that ever walked!

There was a silence unlike any he'd heard before.

His mother sat upright in the bed, swung her feet out from the sleeping bag and walked across to the other side of the caravan. She didn't look at him as she passed, just went and knelt down at her own bed. The backs of her knees creased. Her head bowed.

Give us this day our daily bread, he said viciously.

You go to sleep, young man. I'll deal with you tomorrow. You'll not be going anywhere for a while, not kayaking nor nothing else.

He didn't stir from the table. She finished her prayers and climbed into her bed in the vast and attentive silence.

He whispered the line again, Fuck the Queen, loud enough that she might hear, but she had turned her face away. He could hear the sobs into the hood of the sleeping bag, and he said aloud that he was sorry, but she didn't turn.

A half hour later he said it again—Sorry, Mammy—but she had fallen asleep.

He reached out and began to mold another piece of bread and the hours slid forward and by morning he had made two chess teams—one white, the other the brown of cocoa—just two pieces missing.

AFTER THREE DAYS he was allowed out again and he ran down to the house, but there was no sign of them in the front, so he stole around to the side window. The old man was napping. His wife sat at a mirror. The boy could see her reflection. There were brown freckles in the glass and she kept shifting her head sideways in order to avoid them. Between her neck cords there was a deep hollow. Her skin seemed corrugated and her eyes were a startling green. She took off her housecoat and the boy ducked his head, and when he looked a second time, she already had her nightdress on. She climbed into the bed and leaned across the old man, reached for a book, and momentarily both their bodies merged into one.

The boy moved away from the house and spat on the ground where the sunlight hit shadow.

THE WIND CAME UP from the sea as if it were looking for someone. It was the fifty-first day and he had heard that another hunger striker was critically ill and his uncle in the prison hospital was having a hard time focusing his vision, that everything was blurry. A prison guard had come and taunted him with binoculars. There were jokes being made about very thin coffins. His uncle was lying on a sheepskin blanket now to protect his skin, and he had been moved to a waterbed to keep away the sores. The boy imagined what his body might look like: the chest caved in, his arms thin, his hipbones showing through his pajamas. He was unable to walk now, and there were prison orderlies who wheeled him around. Sometimes the orderlies, even though they were Protestants, would bring him tobacco, which was only worsening his cough. He was allowed to sit outside in the prison hospital courtyard for an hour each day, and despite the warm weather his uncle wrapped himself in half a dozen blankets. He liked to make bets with others in the hospital on when certain crows would leave the razor wire of the prison. He had sent out a statement saying he wasn't afraid of death because it was a cause worth his life.

The boy began to think that death was a thi̇
the living carried with them. He remembered a poem from
school. *Death once dead there's no more dying then*. The line
shot around in his mouth as he slumped through town.

Kayaking kept the thoughts away. The world was altered
from the position of water. In the repetition there was quiet-
ness. He could feel his arms strengthening and a small knot
of muscle growing harder at his neck. His back felt tight
and powerful. Even his knees no longer protested at the
ache. He checked the size of his biceps against the black
armband that he wore.

The old Lithuanian allowed him a stint at the rear of the
kayak, where most of the movement was controlled, and he
made deliberate mistakes so the boy would correct them.
The boat went sideways right and he pulled harder left. The
old man leaned over so the boy would learn how to use the
paddle to steady the boat. Out beyond the harbor, they went
sideways into a series of low waves from a passing speed-
boat and for a moment they surfed along a rush of water
until hit by another wave and the boat felt as if it would
overturn, but the boy turned the boat bow first into the
waves and the Lithuanian nodded his approval.

The boy sensed he had achieved a rhythm with the old
man, that there was some invisible axle that joined them,

making their arms rotate at the same time; they were part of the same machinery, and together they were distancing themselves from all other machines. He thought of cogs clicking into the handiwork of the sea, meeting at the right moment, noiselessly. They worked in unison and their paddles didn't clash in the air and it struck the boy that the air between them was charged with mystery.

Far out, they turned, found shelter in a cove where seals barked on the rocks, and stopped paddling and let the boat drift. The water lapped gently against the side of the boat and the seals barked farther down the shore.

The old man smoked and when the cigarette was finished the boy secretly picked the butt out of the water and put it in his pocket to dry out. He let his paddle float and put his arms behind his head and wondered aloud about what sort of power it might take to club a seal to death.

There's not much worth dying for, said the old man.

What?

Especially if you're a seal, he chuckled.

But the boy thought he was talking of something beyond seals, and all of a sudden he felt an anger and he said bitterly: Why did you come here?

Oh, I really don't think about these things anymore.

Why not?

Because it's easier not to.

I'd love to club a seal to death, said the boy.

The sun shone down a hard yellow and wheels of light worked on the water's edge. The boy's paddle struck the water and moved the boat forward slightly. The old man accepted the anger and leaned into the toil of paddling out of the cove. The wind was at their backs and the boat moved quickly. They brought it parallel to the headland and then swung with ease into the harbor, both the boy and the man silent.

When they got to the pier the boy spat in the water and then put his finger to his nose and let out a stream of snot. The old man gave a small chuckle.

At the pierside the old woman asked them if they were all right. They each nodded and she laughed, distilling the tension. She had brought them lettuce and tomato sandwiches and she brandished them in the air, a grin on her face.

When they sat at the edge of the pier she put her arm around the boy's shoulder and said she was glad that her husband had a partner to take to the water with.

He's got a new happiness, said the woman.

The boy looked at her from under a stray lock of hair.

We never had any children, she said.

The old man coughed and gave her a hard look but she just smiled back.

You look tanned, she said to the boy, and he touched his face as if it didn't belong to him.

He was taken to the house and was surprised by their poverty. She wore a pale housedress and her slippers were made from worn carpet. A ratty sofa had stuffing peeping out. The tasseled runner on a piano was frayed. An empty birdcage hung from the ceiling and the slatted light from the torn window blinds showed the walls in need of paint.

The woman heated a bowl of strange-tasting soup, and when she handed him the cup, he noticed a milky foulness to her breath. She gave him a round piece of bread with a hole in the middle, like a doughnut. She called it a *baronka* and she said that in some places it was called a bagel. She had baked it herself and it was fresh in his mouth and he wondered what sort of chess set he could make from it. He stretched his toes out to the electric bar heater which stood in front of the fireplace. It gave out an uneven heat. Two fire irons and a poker were arranged in front of the fireplace and he wondered why they didn't light a real fire, and when he asked, the old man said there was a family of swifts that lived in the chimney and he didn't want to burn them out. He explained that, when he and his wife first moved in, it had seemed to him that the flue was singing.

When the soup was finished the woman asked him if he had enjoyed the meal. The bread was nice but it was the worst soup the boy had ever tasted in his life, yet still he told her it was lovely and she smiled at him and retreated to an old oak swivel chair. She twirled in it and hummed a little tune to herself. He noticed that her housedress was thin at the elbows, but she wore a couple of thick fancy bracelets on her wrist.

There was a long silence between the three of them until the woman stood up and took the boy's hand and examined the beginnings of the tattoo he had put on his forefinger. She said something quick and guttural in her language to her husband and then she touched the boy's hair.

You shouldn't do that, she said.

She looked at him strangely, and the old man nodded and tore at his bread with his teeth. The boy thought there must be a secret between them. She leaned back in her chair and her mind seemed to go elsewhere. The boy examined photos on the mantelpiece and watched the sweep of the pendulum in an ancient clock.

A high hard feeling of emptiness hit his stomach and he put his teacup down on the table and asked to be excused. The old woman rose and escorted him to the door, took his hand, ran her finger over the unfinished tattoo, and leaned toward him.

Your uncle I heard about, she said. I hope everything will be okay.

Thanks.

When you get older, she said, you will learn that pain is not much of a surprise. Do you understand?

I do, aye.

He turned away slightly and she kissed him high on the side of his head.

You're a good boy, she said.

He felt frightened as he ran down the pathway past roses in bloom, and when he was far away from the house he rubbed at the place where she had kissed him. He thought it was as if he were both inside and outside their happiness, as if he could step back and forth between them, liking and hating them in equal amounts, a paddle hitting either side of the water.

He spent the day walking through the town, and at the newsstand he stole a paper that was full of news articles but no mention of his uncle's name. There was an editorial that said the hunger strike was the equivalent of a freezing man lighting fire to himself for warmth, and he tried to understand this but he couldn't, so he torched the paper by the rear wall of the handball alley and scrunched his toes into the embers.

THE RIOTS BACK HOME were full-scale now. Some prison guards had been shot. Two joyriders had been gunned down in Twinbrook. A young girl, bringing home milk, had been hit in the head with a rubber bullet and she was in a coma. Somebody had slit the throats of a whole herd of cattle because they belonged to a Catholic farmer and the herd had been strung together to make the word NO in the field. He tried to imagine it, the dead cattle, end to end, their tails in the blood of another one's throat.

He began thinking of it all as some chess game and he was at the front of it, a small piece moving, heading toward the end of the board, which could have been a pier or a cliff face or any other part of the town.

The back seam of his left shoe was split now, and when he moved it opened and closed rhythmically. In the abandoned car above the cove he thought about kicking in the last window but lay down instead on the back seat and put his head against the door frame, woke startled to see a stray horse staring in at him. The nostrils of the horse flared and then it shook its head, neighed, and galloped away. The boy was sure he had seen his uncle's spirit and he ran back along the headland and burst breathlessly into the caravan. The door banged loudly. The radio was on. His mother looked up from where she was writing songs in her notebook and simply shook her head, no.

Fifty-five   114.4 lbs   52 kg   100/40   I don't suppose
                          exactly   he has much left.

IN THE MORNING she was at the table, her legs drawn up on the chair. She had made pancakes for him. He noticed that her eyes were puffy and she looked older than ever before. She had not dyed her hair for two months and there were a couple of stray pieces of gray at her temple. She was staring down out the caravan window.

It'll be okay, Mammy, he said.

She looked up at him and smiled.

It'll all work out, he said.

Pardon me?

Don't you worry, Mammy.

She said he was sounding more and more like his father these days and he even had the same cheeky tone of voice.

Oh, he used to do the silliest things, she said. He once stood on his head and drank a full bottle of Coke. And another time he made a lopsided table that he liked to read at, can you imagine that? All the legs were different lengths, and depending where you put the pressure it would move up and down like a boat on the sea.

Why?

For devilment, she said. He was a real joker. He used to play all sorts of tricks. He put glue on a wooden spoon one day and I couldn't shake it off my hand; he found it hilarious.

I'm not a joker though.

Aye, but you're a funny wee lad.

You said *wee*!

I did, aye.

They sat at the table, both of them cutting up the pancakes into smaller and smaller pieces.

Oh, your poor grandmother, she said suddenly, your poor, poor grandmother.

The boy had no idea what he should say. To make her happy he poured some syrup on the pancakes and ate them with as much relish as he possibly could. The syrup tasted exceedingly sweet and he washed it down with quick mouthfuls of tea. For a moment he felt he might vomit.

His mother drew her legs up into her chest so her chin rested on her kneecap.

What'll we do today? she asked.

We could hitch a lift and go shopping in Galway, he said.

We could.

Or maybe we could go for a swim.

That's a great idea, she said. That's the best idea you ever had in your life.

She dragged him up from the chair by his hand, stuffed their swimsuits and a couple of towels in a white plastic bag. She pushed open the door of the caravan and instead of going toward the town she went east along the headland, past the abandoned Vauxhall, bounding over a series of boulders. She held his hand and laughed and when they got near the shoreline she hunkered down behind a giant rock and switched into her black swimsuit. Her skin was pale as candle wax against it.

Last in's a rotten egg, she shouted as she stepped gingerly over the rocks into the water.

The waves came up to her and broke at the waist and it seemed to him like the opening of hands. She waded out until the water was above her breasts and she dipped beneath the surface. She came up twenty yards away and waved at him.

He hid behind a different rock and pulled on his trunks. She was already churning a line out on the water when he followed her into the widening vee of her wake. He was a quicker swimmer than she and soon he caught up and swam past her. She treaded water and splashed him. He began splashing back, and soon they were both laughing.

He ducked underwater and swam in the salty darkness away from her. He looked on the water for the kayak but it was nowhere in sight.

They swam for fifteen minutes and then they walked back up the hillside together, chatting about a song she was writing about seagulls and the way they dipped for food. She hummed a little of it and asked him what he thought of the melody and he said it was wonderful. She explained she was going to dedicate the song to his uncle and the boy put his arm around his mother's shoulders. He felt his fingers grip the top of her shoulder. She bent her head sideways and leaned on him.

You're getting fierce big, she said.

He helped her up the hillside and as they walked he thought to himself that his childhood had all of a sudden fallen away, that he had dropped it like a skin in the sea.

HE CHALLENGED HER to a game, the rules being that they had to eat each piece when it was taken. In seven moves he deliberately lost his queen. He went to the fridge and took out the butter and a pot of strawberry jam. He pasted some onto the chess piece for her and this time, when she said it was delicious, he didn't get angry, and they sat there until all the pieces were eaten, except for the kings and her pawn.

Stalemate, he said.

He didn't flinch when she patted his hand.

It'll be today or tomorrow, she said.

I know.

That's the worst thing, isn't it? she said. Just knowing. How inevitable it is.

You never know, Mammy.

It's hard to believe isn't it?

It is, aye.

You know what? I wouldn't mind being on my own for a minute, pet.

Aye, surely.

He made another chess set and went down to the town and knocked on the old man's door. He had forgotten to ask the Lithuanian if he had ever played chess but he felt sure he would. After rapping six times on the door he kicked it once with his foot, but there was still nobody home. He thought about trying to break in to see if there were any cigarettes left lying around, but there were fishermen out on the pier and they were watching him.

He shoved his hands into his pockets and carried the

chess pieces with him through town bouncing around in a small plastic bag. An idea occurred to him and he began to leave individual pieces in various places—a castle that he dropped in the postbox, a bishop that he put in the bank vault, a series of four pawns that he ranged along the wall of the handball alley, a queen he left on the weighing scales outside the chemist's, and two knights, which he left on the top of the pierside bollards. He scanned the water for the kayak but it was nowhere to be seen. Feeling hungry, he ate the remaining pieces.

When the kayak broke the harbor waters he pretended not to see it, just sat with his legs dangling over the pier.

The old man came up behind him and said: Hey there.

The boy didn't reply.

Rasa felt good today and she hasn't been out in the boat for so long, we thought it would be good for her to get out in the sun.

Aye.

I'm sorry we didn't wait for you.

No problem.

I hope you're not angry.

No.

Would you like some soup?

No.

It's terrible, isn't it? The old man laughed. She's the world's worst cook. You know, I married her before I knew her cooking.

The boy turned and tried a smile.

We'll see you tomorrow?

Aye.

Your uncle?

He's grand.

The Lithuanian laid a hand on his shoulder. You're a strong boy.

Thanks.

Tomorrow?

Aye, tomorrow.

He watched the old man and his wife carry the boat up to the house and he heard their muffled voices as they bounced off the well of the boat.

He had rescued a few cigarette butts along the pier and he took them from his pocket. There was one with lipstick, which he smoked with relish. He wondered if his uncle was still smoking even at this stage of the strike, the sixty-first day, and then the boy closed his eyes to a specific vision— his uncle under a fluorescent light, lying there supine, eyes wide and staring, prison nurses thin-lipped above him, drip bags waiting as an argument against the last rites, no feeling in his legs or arms or fingers or toes, bones jutting out horribly against his chest, his heart beating dull against his skin, his body feeding on the protein of his brain now.

The boy wiped at his tears and shouted out at the sea, and in a long string, cursed every curse he knew. Behind him he could hear the church bells ringing and he knew his mother would be worried, but he sat on the pier and didn't move.

SHE CAME JUST BEFORE SUNSET and he watched her in the phone box. She nodded at whatever news was coming over the line. He resented the tight magenta blouse that she wore. He felt certain she would be angry at him for staying out all day, but when she put down the phone she walked across and sat down beside him and said there was no change.

Today or tomorrow, she said.

She used the same tone of voice that she used for her prayers. The boy remembered the prayer she incanted frequently, finishing with the words: *After this our exile.*

They watched the sun disappear on the horizon. It was a magnificent red and it seemed to spill itself out generously into the sky. The seagulls let out thin and labored squalls as they defiled low over the pier. The water lapped gray against the stonework. The boy thought there was a loneliness to everything in the world. His mother turned and held his hand briefly and told him to make sure he was home before night fell.

THE DARKNESS WAS COMPLETE and already a couple of stars had risen in the east.

He stopped for a long time by the pierside phone. The ring came high and hard. The receiver vibrated on its hook. He opened the door of the booth and the wind moved the coiled wire. His hand hovered in midair and then he decided against answering it. It sounded as if the phone itself were mourning. Soon his mother would come down from the caravan and hear it and she would answer and then he would know for definite. He found himself shaking and he lowered his chin to his chest when the ringing stopped.

He stole around the side of the house and peeped into the window and saw the Lithuanian couple sleeping, back to back.

The woman's hair was unloosed and a few strands had fallen across her husband's face. The old man seemed gigantic beside her.

The boy could still feel her kiss from days ago on his head like a stigmata. His chin felt cold against the pane of glass. He dipped away from the window and went around the side of the house.

The boat was easy to handle without the paddles and he lifted it by the lip of the well with just one arm and negotiated the short driveway, snagging it once on a rosebush.

It felt light with his new strength.

He dragged the kayak behind him onto the beach and stood a long time looking out to sea, the phosphorescent waves rolling onto the sand like brothers. There were no boats out on the water and the sea was a deep black. His blood was racing. Dizzy, he turned and walked up the beach to the life preserver pole, propped the kayak up against it. He steadied the bow in the sand and then used the rope to tie the boat to the pole. His fingers trembled but still he made a tight knot. The kayak stood against the pole like a misshapen man and there was a dapple of birdshit where the mouth should be. He sat down and stared at it for a while, tried to calm his hands.

The phone rang again in the distance. He rose and walked the beach, looking over his shoulder at the kayak, until he found some large rocks at the very front of the pier.

He carted the rocks down and made a large pile at his feet. He lifted the first one high and felt the shudder in his body as he hurled it toward the kayak. He was surprised at the arc of the rock, confused that it had come from his fingers. It hit the boat with a loud thud, bounced back, and threw up a flume of sand where it landed. He bit his lip and hurled another.

A rim of moon hung in the sky. The wind chilled his arms. The tide moved insistently.

He picked up a larger rock and flung it, and again it just bounced away from the kayak and he cursed the boat's resilience. He went close to it and bashed a rock repeatedly at one point until a tiny hairline crack developed. Combing the beach again he found even larger rocks. His whole body was trembling now. He was on a street. He was at a funeral. He had a bottle of fire in his hands. He was in a prison cell. He pushed a plate away from his bedside.

It was only with the twelfth rock and another long ringing of the phone that he saw at last the spidery splint of fiberglass.

A jolt of adrenaline hit his stomach as he neared the boat. He began to hit it with his fists until blood appeared on his knuckles, and then he rested his head against the coolness of the kayak and he cried.

When his sobs subsided the boy lifted his head from the boat, looked back over his shoulder, saw the light from the house of the Lithuanians, the front door open, the couple standing together, hands clasped, the old man's eyes squinting, the woman's large and tender.